D1208400

THE CLUE OF THE SILVER SCORPION

KEN HOLT *Mystery Stories*

THE SECRET OF SKELETON ISLAND

THE RIDDLE OF THE STONE ELEPHANT

THE BLACK THUMB MYSTERY

THE CLUE OF THE MARKED CLAW

THE CLUE OF THE COILED COBRA

THE SECRET OF HANGMAN'S INN

THE MYSTERY OF THE IRON BOX

THE CLUE OF THE PHANTOM CAR

THE MYSTERY OF THE GALLOPING HORSE

THE MYSTERY OF THE GREEN FLAME

THE MYSTERY OF THE GRINNING TIGER

THE MYSTERY OF THE VANISHING MAGICIAN

THE MYSTERY OF THE SHATTERED GLASS

THE MYSTERY OF THE INVISIBLE ENEMY

THE MYSTERY OF GALLOWS CLIFF

THE CLUE OF THE SILVER SCORPION

"Stop right where you are!" the man commanded

A KEN HOLT Mystery

THE CLUE
OF THE SILVER
SCORPION

By Bruce Campbell

GROSSET & DUNLAP *Publishers*

NEW YORK

CONTENTS

CHAPTER		PAGE
I	TURNPIKE THIEF	1
II	BOOBY TRAP	19
III	SANDY SCENTS A LINK	35
IV	BOOMERANG	58
V	HELPLESS	74
VI	KEN BLUNDERS	96
VII	RACE AGAINST MINUTES	112
VIII	CORNERED	132
IX	A TRAP IS SPRUNG	144
X	TAKING STOCK	164

THE CLUE OF THE SILVER SCORPION

CHAPTER I

TURNPIKE THIEF

THE two young men paused briefly before opening the glass-paneled door on which were lettered the words: STEVEN GRANGER, MANAGER.

"Batten down the hatches, Ken," Sandy Allen advised. The big redhead was more than six feet tall, with a breadth of shoulders to match his height. The hand he closed around the doorknob engulfed it completely.

Ken Holt, slimmer and half a head shorter than his friend, grinned up at him. "And reef the sails," he added. "Go on, Sandy. Open it."

Sandy Allen twisted the knob silently. Ken had followed him into the room beyond before the stocky gray-haired man at the battered desk looked up.

"I might have known it!" Granger's hoarse voice had the rasp of a file. "Here I am—manager of the eastern division of one of the world's largest news

1

services—and I can't even be protected from riff-raff barging in uninvited!"

Ken bowed from the waist. "How do you do, sir? I'm Riff." He gestured toward Sandy. "Meet my friend, Raff."

"You two lazy would-be newsmen!" Granger growled. "Get out of here and let a working member of the press work." Then a look of concern swiftly replaced the mock anger in his face. "Anything wrong?" he asked. "You two in trouble?"

"Of course not!" Ken assured him, as if the possibility were too remote to consider. "We're in town to pick up a birthday present for Sandy's father," he went on, speaking in his normal voice for the first time. "We bought him an eighteenth-century dragoon's pistol for his gun collection. So we thought we'd just drop by here to find out when Dad is due back and—"

"Week from next Friday," Granger interrupted briskly. "At least that's the date he gave me. But how often does your foot-loose father turn up when he's supposed to? He filed his last cable on the London trade conference yesterday. That should mean he's in Paris by now, on his way to Algiers and then Casablanca and then home. But of course I'm only his editor." He sighed. "He couldn't be expected to let me know if he went off following the whiff of some good story."

"And naturally that sort of thing upsets you pretty

badly," Sandy said, with an air of false sympathy. "Global News just hates to get the kind of exclusive news beats Dick Holt sends in all the time."

Granger grinned and ran his fingers through his unruly hair. "That's right," he agreed. "It makes us uncomfortable to be the envy of all the other news services. Now if that's all you two are here for—" He looked meaningfully at his cluttered desk.

"That's all," Ken said. "Except for our reward, of course," he added casually.

"Reward!" Granger sat up straighter. "What did you two ever do to earn a reward? You're lucky I pay you for those worthless stories and fuzzy pictures you send in here. What more do you want?"

"Only what we were promised," Sandy told him. "But of course if you've got such a short memory—" He turned to Ken. "You wouldn't think he could forget, would you, that only three short days ago he was down on his knees, pleading with tears in his eyes?"

"No, you wouldn't," Ken agreed, shaking his head sadly. "I remember it so clearly myself. 'Get me Macready's picture and an interview, boys,' he said, 'and you can have anything you want!' None of his regular staff had been able to reach Macready. He turned to us in despair."

"And we," Sandy picked it up, "with the genius that always characterizes our work—"

"And with a slight assist from your brother Bert,

who happened to go to college with Macready's son," Ken inserted softly.

". . . broke down Macready's negative attitude toward the press and achieved the impossible," Sandy concluded.

Granger was grinning. "So that's how you managed it!" he said. "Bert fixed it for you!"

Ken and Sandy ignored him.

"But does the cruel editor remember now what he told us at the triumphant moment when we gave him what he had long sought in vain?" Ken demanded. "Ah, no. He forgets he promised us four box seats for Friday's double-header, so that Pop and Bert and you and I—"

Granger was pulling open the drawer of his desk. "I would have been crazy to promise you any such thing. After all, the Macready assignment was routine. Anybody could have handled it. But by a strange coincidence I happen to have four seats for the double-header right here, which I'm not going to be able to use myself. So you might as well take them." He tossed an envelope at Ken.

The boys grinned at each other when they saw that the envelope had already been addressed to them, in care of Pop Allen's *Brentwood Advance*, Brentwood, New Jersey.

"And he's even put a stamp on it," Ken said. "You know, Sandy, I feel sorry for Granger sometimes. He hates to spend money, and we've forced him to waste this perfectly good stamp by coming in here today. I don't think we can accept it, do you?"

"Absolutely not," Sandy agreed.

Ken opened the envelope, took out the four tickets, and put them in his pocket. "Here, sir," he said, putting the envelope on Granger's desk. "We'd feel better if you'd let us return this to you."

"And I'd feel better if you two would get out of my office," Granger growled.

"We were just leaving, weren't we, Raff?" Ken said.

"That we were, Riff," Sandy agreed.

"And about time." Granger reached for his pencil and bent over the stack of copy on his desk. "I was going to cable your father tonight anyway, Ken," he said, without looking up. "I'll remind him about Pop Allen's birthday. Maybe that'll bring him home on time."

"Thanks," Ken said. "And for these, too." His hand touched the pocket where he had put the tickets.

"Yes, sir. Thanks a lot," Sandy echoed.

Granger appeared not to have heard them.

Quietly the boys let themselves out.

"What a man," Sandy murmured, as they walked past a battery of clacking news tickers. "Do you suppose he ever fools anybody with that growling-bear act?"

"Not for long," Ken said. "I'm sure there isn't a reporter in New York who doesn't want to work for him. Or anywhere else, for that matter," he added. "I remember Dad saying he's met newsmen all over the world who wished they could get on the Global News staff just so they could work under Steve Granger."

He glanced at his watch. "It's only three fifteen. We'll be home in time for supper, after all."

"Sure we will." They had reached the bank of elevators in the hall and stood waiting for a down car. "Especially," Sandy went on, "as I was planning to make only one stop on the way. For a little solid nourishment to keep up our strength."

"Only one!" Ken looked at him in mock amazement.

Sandy nodded firmly. "The rest of the way I plan to starve myself. Except for maybe a chocolate bar or two."

"You really think you'll survive an ordeal like that?" Ken asked, as an elevator door clanged open and they stepped inside. "Remember we're over fifty miles from Brentwood—and you're planning to do it on just one real meal and a few tidbits. I doubt if you'll pull through."

Sandy clenched his teeth and lifted his chin. "You'll see," he promised. "Not another morsel shall pass my lips until we get home. Unless we run into a traffic jam," he added quickly, "and get held up for ten or fifteen minutes."

"Naturally," Ken said. "In an emergency like that

you would have to revise your schedule, or risk certain death."

The elevator discharged most of its passengers on the ground floor. Only the boys remained inside as it dropped another floor to the basement.

Ken was in the lead as they walked along the corridor that lead to the underground garage. With a thrust of his arm he pushed the heavy fire door that opened into the parking space.

A startled grunt reached his ears as he stepped through into the big dusky area, crowded with rows of cars. He realized that a man, standing just inside the door, had been knocked off balance by his push. Ken saw the figure bent forward, right arm outflung.

"Sorry!" Ken said, reaching out a steadying hand.

But the man had already straightened. Ken's fingers merely brushed a large envelope clamped under the stranger's left arm and knocked it to the floor. "I'm sorry!" Ken repeated, bending for the envelope.

"I'll get it," the man said quickly, and snatched it up from the dusty floor. "It was my fault," he added hurriedly. "I shouldn't have been standing in the way. But there seems to be some confusion over there at the garage entrance and I was just waiting here until—er—it cleared up."

"Confusion?" Ken repeated questioningly. He looked over at the ramp and saw two cars waiting at the foot of it.

Sandy, behind him, muttered, "There's our car—between those two Global trucks. Let's have the attendant ease it out so we don't find ourselves with a bill from Global for a couple of imaginary fender dents."

"All right," Ken agreed absent-mindedly. "There's the attendant talking to those two cops over there by the ramp. What seems to be the trouble?" he asked the stranger beside him.

"What? Er—I'm not sure." The man had a thin neck and his Adam's apple rose and fell in it convulsively. "The police just seem to be holding up the cars. That's all I know."

Ken groaned. "This means you're going to want to stop twice for food on the way home," he told Sandy.

Sandy was grinning. "Let's go over and see what's going on," he said. "Wouldn't it be a joke if the garage had been robbed and Granger didn't know about it? A crime right under his nose—and he doesn't get the story until a couple of Brentwood reporters let him in on it! Come on."

He had already started across the floor. Ken made a gesture of farewell to the man he had almost knocked down and moved after his friend.

But before they could question either of the two policemen near the ramp, one of the officers snapped, "Who are you?"

The boys gave him their names, and showed him their drivers' licenses as identification.

"What's up?" Sandy asked, as the man grunted his satisfaction and they returned their wallets to their pockets.

"Attempted bank robbery over on the next street," the policeman answered shortly.

"And you think the man may be hiding in here?" Ken asked.

"Could be," the officer replied. "Anyway we're searching this place, along with the rest of the neighborhood. See anybody as you came through the garage?" he added quickly.

Ken hesitated. "Just one man," he admitted. "Tall, thin, middle-aged—"

The policeman interrupted him. "Forget it," he said. "We're looking for a short, heavy-set chap—gray-haired."

"You know," Sandy said helpfully, "this ramp isn't the only way out of here. There's a door over there—the one we came through—that—"

"And you know, bud," the officer cut in scathingly, "if you try to get out that way now, you'd find a guard there checking everybody who leaves the garage."

"Oh," Sandy said.

Ken hid his grin. "May we take our car out of here now, Officer?" he asked politely.

"There's the lieutenant," the policeman informed them. "Ask him."

A third uniformed man, wearing a lieutenant's

insignia, had come out of the attendant's office, and was inspecting the first of the two cars halted at the foot of the ramp.

"I'll speak to him," Ken said quietly to Sandy. "And if it's O.K. for us to leave I'll ask the attendant to bring the car out. You go ahead and call Granger and let him know the Global News basement is the scene of a rigorous police search."

"Right." Sandy, recovered from the policeman's snub, grinned briefly before he turned away toward a telephone booth against the garage wall. Ken started toward the police lieutenant, driver's license once more in hand.

Half an hour later, on the New Jersey side of the Holland Tunnel, Sandy slowed their red convertible to a stop long enough to accept a toll ticket at the entrance to the Jersey Turnpike. When he got the car in motion again he grinned. "Next stop a restaurant," he announced. "And in the meantime you can look in the glove compartment and see what the situation is in regard to chocolate bars or other forms of sustenance."

"I'm not surprised by your request," Ken told him resignedly. "To be frank, I didn't expect you to get out of New York without stopping to eat. We must have been held up at least seven minutes in the Global News garage. And you'd finished a measly four-course meal at least two hours before. If you feel too faint to drive," he added, "I'll be glad to—"

"Never mind the fancy insults," Sandy told him. "Find me a chocolate bar."

Ken snapped open the glove compartment and reached in to feel around among the jumble of maps and small tools that seemed to fill it to overflowing.

"Try the far right corner," Sandy suggested. "I'm pretty sure I—" He broke off with a laugh as half a dozen maps slid forward onto the floor of the car.

Ken shot him a disgusted look before he bent over to pick up the maps. "Next time look for your own chocolate bar," he muttered. "And when we get home remind me to throw out half the stuff in here," he went on, a moment later. "Look at these." He held the maps up so that Sandy could take a quick glance at them. "One of these rare documents is a torn map of New Jersey. And here's one of New England that we must have picked up last year. Don't we ever clean this thing out and get rid of the stuff that's out of date?"

Ken began to separate the items in his hand into two groups. "This can go," he said. "And this."

"Don't throw that one out—the blue one!" Sandy said hastily. "That's the map of San Francisco we used when we were there with your father. I want to keep it as a souvenir. We certainly had a great time out there," he added reminiscently.

"There are moments of that trip—before we finally landed in San Francisco—that I'd just as soon forget," Ken said.

They both fell silent then for a time, thinking back to the dangers they had encountered in the adventure Granger had tagged *The Mystery of Gallows Cliff*. Then Ken found his mind slipping still farther into the past, back to the first adventure he and Sandy had been involved in together—the one they sometimes called *The Secret of Skeleton Island*. That was the time when Ken had first met the redheaded Allen clan—Pop, Pop's older son, Bert, and Mom Allen, as tiny as her husband and sons were huge— and Sandy himself. When the Allens had learned that Ken was motherless, they had practically adopted him. And he shared in the work and excitement of operating their weekly newspaper, the *Brentwood Advance*. For a long time now even Ken's father had considered the Allen house his real home, on those rare occasions when his work permitted him a few days of leisure.

There had been many shared adventures since that first one. And Granger had bought accounts more than once, in the form of stories by Ken and photographs by Sandy. Granger had even been heard to say that the boys had the makings of first-class newsmen—a form of praise the Global News editor seldom expressed. Pop Allen, an equally hard taskmaster, had admitted that Granger might be right. "Though it's too soon to tell," he had added hastily, eying the boys over his blackened pipe.

Sandy's voice roused Ken from his thoughts. "Forget the chocolate bar!" he announced. "There's a restaurant up ahead!"

Ken grinned at him, shuffled the maps into a single pile again, and pushed them all back into the glove compartment. A few minutes later they were both climbing onto stools at the counter of the roadside restaurant.

"Apple pie and a glass of milk, please," Sandy told the waitress who came toward them.

"Want ice cream on the pie?" she asked.

Sandy looked surprised. "Of course! Vanilla," he added.

"The same for me—but without the ice cream," Ken said.

The waitress moved away and Ken reached for the water glass she had put down before him. As he did so he glanced into the long mirror which ran the full length of the wall on the other side of the counter, and which reflected part of the parking lot beyond the restaurant's glass-walled front.

"Look!" Ken was already off his stool and heading for the door. "Somebody's trying to get into our car!"

Sandy was at his side by the time he reached the door, and together they ran along the aisle that separated two rows of parked cars. Their own convertible was at the far end of the row on the right, close to the highway. Before they reached it they had to dodge around a family approaching the restaurant. Then, still fifty feet from their goal, they were delayed again by a truck that backed out abruptly into the aisle, closing it off temporarily. Almost a full minute elapsed between the time Ken had leaped from his stool and the moment when they arrived breathless beside the car. And during that period the car had been invisible to them for many seconds.

"There's nobody here now," Sandy said unnecessarily, staring around. "Are you sure what you saw wasn't just somebody walking past the car?"

Ken scratched his head. "I thought I was sure," he said dubiously. "But I guess, now that I think about it, all I really saw was the top of a man's head—he was wearing a gray hat—bent over the door handle as if he were trying to pick the lock. I suppose he *could* have been just walking between these two cars, and stopped because he dropped something."

Sandy bent down and examined the lock's chromium surface. "No sign of any attempt to force it," he murmured. "But if somebody really was here he might have seen us coming, and left too soon to get anywhere with the job." He pulled his keys out of his pocket and unlocked the door. "While we're out here I might as well put my camera gear out of sight in the luggage compartment, along with Pop's present. If anybody was really trying to get into the car it was probably because he saw my stuff. I ought to know better than to leave it out in plain sight like this."

Ken helped him transfer his cases, and they made

certain the now apparently empty car was locked again before they started back toward the restaurant.

The waitress was about to remove the plates of pie she had set at their places. "Thought you'd run out on me," she said.

"I've never run away from a piece of pie in my life," Sandy assured her.

"It was my fault," Ken explained apologetically. "I thought I saw somebody trying to break into our car out there, and we ran out to investigate."

The waitress's eyes widened. "Somebody broke into your car?" she repeated. "In broad daylight! Why, that's never happened before in the three years I've worked here. You'd better report it to the manager."

"I just said I *thought* I saw somebody," Ken repeated. "But I guess I was mistaken. Anyway, we couldn't find any sign of damage on the lock, and the car was still closed."

"Oh. I see." The waitress began to collect the used dishes left behind by a group of departing diners. "I guess you were mistaken, all right," she said cheerfully. "A thief would have to want something pretty badly to break into a car right out there where anybody could see him."

"I guess so," Ken agreed, and applied himself to his pie.

Five minutes later Sandy swallowed the last bite of his food and slid off his stool. "That was fine," he told the waitress. "Now I can hold out until—" He broke off suddenly. "He's there again!" he told Ken, and sprinted for the door.

Ken swung around. From where he sat he could see no one near their car. But Sandy was through the door now and running down the aisle between the parked rows.

Ken glanced at the money he had already taken out of his pocket, dropped it on the counter, and started for the door himself. "Keep the change," he called back over his shoulder to the waitress who was staring after him in amazement.

When he reached their red convertible he found an angry Sandy fingering a six-inch slit in the canvas top.

"Look at that!" the redhead said furiously. "He thought he could get his arm through here and release the lock from inside! You were certainly right, Ken. We never should have left the car after you saw him the first time. But I didn't really believe you, you know. I thought—"

"I know," Ken said. "I figured I'd been mistaken myself. After all, it doesn't make sense. In broad daylight, as the waitress said, a thief would be running a big risk."

"But why would he want to break into the car, anyway?" Sandy demanded. "Especially now, with my camera stuff locked up in the luggage compartment."

Sandy angrily fingered a six-inch slit
in the canvas top

"I suppose he hoped to steal the car," Ken said slowly.

"But that doesn't make sense either!" Sandy protested. "He could never expect to get off the turnpike without getting caught. The minute we reported the theft, all the exits would be checked. Why, he wouldn't stand a chance in the world of getting away with it!"

"Well, what do you think he was after then?" Ken asked.

"It's got me stumped," Sandy admitted. "Absolutely and utterly stumped."

"Me too," Ken agreed.

They looked at each other, and then they turned to look at the gash in the convertible's neat top. Ken found himself thinking once more of the words of the waitress who had said, "A thief would have to want something pretty badly to break into a car right out there where anybody could see him."

"But what could he have wanted?" he said, half aloud. "What?"

CHAPTER II

BOOBY TRAP

SANDY opened the car door with his key. "At least he didn't ruin the lock," he muttered. "And I suppose our insurance will cover the repair job. But I'd sure like to meet that slit artist face to face for a couple of minutes!"

Ken roused himself. "Did you get a good look at him?" he asked. "What are we standing here for?" he added suddenly. "Maybe we can find him!"

"It's no use trying," Sandy said disgustedly. "All I really saw was his back, in some kind of a dark suit or coat, and that gray hat you spotted before. And I only saw that much from the restaurant. He wasn't in sight while I was running out here—and of course when I got here, and saw the slit, I stopped to look at it instead of starting right off to search the place for somebody in a gray hat. It would have been a long shot, but I should have tried it. It's certainly too late now."

"Yes, I suppose so," Ken agreed.

"Let's go," Sandy said, sliding into the driver's seat. "We're not going to learn anything hanging around here."

Ken reluctantly joined him in the car. "It seems as if there ought to be something we can do," he muttered, "but I don't know what it is."

Sandy pulled out of the parking place and soon they were traveling along the turnpike again. Neither of them spoke for some time.

"The more I think about it," Ken said finally, "the more I think the man must have tried to steal the car. Maybe he was a stranger around here, and didn't know the turnpike exits are all barred by toll booths."

"How did he get out here then?" Sandy asked argumentatively. "You can't reach that restaurant except by the turnpike. And once anybody drives onto the turnpike, he knows about the toll booths because he has to pass one to get on."

"Maybe he was a hitchhiker," Ken suggested.

"They're not permitted on the turnpike," Sandy pointed out.

"He could have come across the fields," Ken reminded him.

"I suppose so," Sandy agreed. "But even a hitchhiker would know that in the middle of the afternoon people aren't likely to stay in a restaurant very long. If he'd waited until dinner hour, when he might think he'd have at least half an hour—" He shook his head. "No, I can't buy that. Unless he was a very stupid hitchhiker," he added, grinning slightly.

"Or a man so smart he was sure nobody would suspect him of trying to steal a car in broad daylight, in the middle of the afternoon," Ken suggested. Then he too shook his head. "No, that doesn't wash, either. He must have seen us running out to the car the first time, when I spotted him. That must be why he took off then. And a smart man wouldn't try to pull the same trick twice on the same car—when he knew we'd spotted him from inside the restaurant the first time."

"Unless he was desperate," Sandy said.

"Desperate for what?" Ken asked.

They glanced at each other and grinned.

"Let's give it up," Sandy suggested. "Neither of us has the slightest idea of what he was trying to do, or why. And we never will."

"I guess not. We'll just have to file it away among 'Unusual Incidents,'" Ken said.

Sandy sighed. "Sometimes I think that practically everything that happens to us is unusual."

When they reached Brentwood they stopped at the *Advance* office to find the linotype machines quiet, the operators gone, and Pop and Bert about to close their desks for the day. Ken showed them the baseball tickets and described their visit to Granger's office, while Sandy unobtrusively dialed the telephone number of the man who handled the insurance on their car.

Bert, who knew the boys' principal reason for going to New York had been the purchase of Pop's present, rallied to Ken's aid by asking questions about Granger. And Pop—who, Ken suspected, had guessed the reason for their trip—also politely pretended that a call on Granger had been their major purpose. But Bert's ears were sharp. He overhead fragments of Sandy's conversation.

"What happened?" Bert asked. "You didn't crack up the convertible, did you?"

"No," Ken said quickly. "Somebody cut a slit in the canvas top—trying to get inside the car, I suppose. It happened when we stopped for some milk and pie on the turnpike."

"And you didn't nab him?" Bert sat up straight from his usual slumped position.

Ken shook his head. "We barely saw him," he said. "All we could tell was that it was somebody in a gray hat."

Bert laughed. "Did you hear that, Pop? A criminal attacks their car, and these two Sherlock Holmeses don't even know who he was—except that he wore a gray hat."

"Let the boy alone, Bert!" Pop ordered. "It could have happened to anyone."

"Any ordinary people," Bert said, grinning widely. "But not to these great criminologists." He turned his fire on his younger brother, who had hung up the phone. The boys had to endure several minutes of further bantering from Bert before Pop cut it off.

"All right—that's enough. As I see it, the only problem is when and how you're going to get your car fixed."

"Mr. Slade told us to take it to Joe Meyers' garage, and send him the bill," Sandy said.

"Good. Then that's that." Pop got to his feet. "And if you're going to take it to Joe's tonight, you'd better get at it. Mom's going to have dinner ready by six, and it's not far from that now. Come on, Bert. At least you and I can be home on time."

Bert got up, too, bundling a pile of notes into his top drawer with one hand in order to clear his desk.

"Look at them, Ken!" Sandy said. "A total of four hundred and fifty pounds of bone and muscle—and afraid of one small woman who can't tip the scales beyond a hundred pounds!"

But Bert refused to rise to Sandy's bait. "Sure, I admit Mom's the boss," he said. "I don't notice you disobeying her orders very often either."

Ken grinned, too. "He's got you there, Sandy. And don't think I'm going to claim I can hold out against Mom," he added quickly. "Tell her we'll be home as soon as we've left the car at the garage," he went on, picking up the phone. "I'll just check with Joe Meyers and make sure he can handle the job if we bring it over now."

Bert tossed a set of keys to Sandy. "I'll go home with Pop," he said. "You'll need my car if you leave yours at the garage."

"Thanks," Sandy said.

"Remember now—don't sit around and talk to Joe half the evening," Pop warned, starting for the back of the shop and the parking space beyond it.

Ken finished his telephone conversation a few seconds after Pop and Bert had disappeared. "Joe says to bring it over right away, so he can get at it the first thing in the morning," he reported.

"Swell. I'll just take my camera stuff out of the back first."

Ken started toward the door with him. "And let's take Pop's present out, too, and put it down in your darkroom. He never goes down there."

Ten minutes later Joe Meyers was inspecting the damage to the convertible's top. His brown eyes narrowed. "Looks as if somebody did this on purpose," he said.

"That's right," Ken agreed. "It happened while we were in a restaurant."

"Mmm. Too bad. But don't worry," Joe said. "There's nothing to it. I'll pull the top off first thing tomorrow and send it over to Halsey's. They'll replace the damaged panel in two shakes of a lamb's tail."

"Swell," Sandy said. "And Mr. Slade said the bill for it should go right to him."

"And we thought you might as well do a lubrication job for us while you've got the car here, Joe," Ken added.

"The whole works, that is," Sandy elaborated. "Oil change, filter, grease job, rotate the tires—"

Joe's wave cut him off. "You don't have to spell it out. Me, I'm in the garage business. You know? I'll check my records and do everything that needs doing. Matter of fact, I'll get started on that right now," he added, getting into the convertible and starting the engine. "I'll have to be around here for an hour more anyway."

"And we ought to be home in three minutes," Ken reminded Sandy. He began to move toward Bert's car, in which he had followed Sandy.

Joe waved and had driven their car into the interior of the garage before they had Bert's car headed out into the street.

The next morning the boys arrived at the office with Bert, to find that Pop had an assignment waiting for them.

"Farm machinery auction," Pop said, around his pipe. "Jed Pollard's stuff. But I want more than an auction story, Ken. Jed's been farming that place all his life, and his father and grandfather before him. Why's he selling off? Get me the whole story. But you won't have to bother to stay through the sale. We can get the details on that later from Wilson."

"The auctioneer, you mean?" Ken asked.

"That's right—Delbert Wilson." Pop nodded.

Sandy had already gone down into his basement darkroom to get the camera equipment he needed. "How many pictures, Pop?"

"Use your own judgment," his father told him. "Just remember I'm more interested in the Pollards, and their story, than the auction itself." He turned his head. "And check with Wilson, Ken, to see if he has many more such auctions lined up for this season. We may have the beginnings of a trend here."

"Right." Ken scribbled a note to himself on the top sheet of his copy paper and thrust it back into his pocket.

"You did say we could use your car—didn't you, Bert?" Sandy asked.

"I did. Reluctantly," Bert answered. "I just wish I were riding out into the country in it today myself, instead of staying here for another of those creamed-chicken-and-peas club luncheons. Take care of it, mind you," he added, as the boys moved toward the shop door. "I don't want it brought back damaged, the way yours was yesterday. What I always say is, people who can't take care of cars really shouldn't be allowed to drive them."

Sandy swung around. "You're a fine one to talk! I remember that time last year when you—"

"Sandy!" His father's roar stopped him. "You've got work to do. Get going!"

"Yes, sir!"

Sandy joined a grinning Ken at the rear door, and they made their way past the two softly clicking linotype machines and the big press. It was motionless now, but David Tanner, the printer, was running supermarket circulars through the smaller press in the corner. He waved as they passed.

Out in the parking lot behind the shop Sandy laid his camera case carefully on the rear seat and slid behind the wheel of Bert's car, not very different from their own except for its color and its hard top.

"I'll drive," he was saying, as Ken got in beside him, "because I remember where the Pollard place is. We go south on the highway about twelve miles and then turn off on a little country road. It wasn't even paved the last time I was on it."

Once out of Brentwood, Sandy let the car pick up speed and it hummed smoothly along the highway.

"I hate to admit it," Sandy said finally, "but Bert takes almost as good care of this thing as we do of ours."

"Even better, you might say," Ken said dryly. "I don't see any slits in his roof." Then he leaned suddenly forward to stare at the gas gauge. "But it won't keep on running like this if we don't put some gas in it. We're lucky there's a filling station up there ahead."

Sandy too looked at the gauge. "Oh, no!" he groaned. "I bet Bert did this on purpose," he muttered, "just so he could get a free tankful of gas.

Well, he's not going to get away with it! We'll collect from him the minute we see him."

"I'm not sure we ought to try," Ken said. "Seems to me I remember your big brother coming home just about a week ago looking mighty irritated. That was the day he'd borrowed our car—and it ran out of gas. As I recall his story, he had to walk four miles through a rainstorm to find a gas station."

"That's right! I'd forgotten about that." Sandy grinned. "I'm glad you reminded me," he added. "Now I can enjoy thinking about it all over again."

Some ten miles beyond the gas station, where they had Bert's tank filled, Sandy slowed down to watch for the road leading off the highway toward the Pollard farm.

They were in no doubt when they reached it. A large sign announcing the auction was posted at the corner.

They had driven only a short distance along the road when they found themselves held up behind a flat, open-bodied farm truck.

"I can't pass him," Sandy muttered. "This road is too narrow and twists too much."

Just then they rounded a corner onto a fairly straight stretch, and realized that there was not just one car ahead of them, but many. All were proceeding at a snail's pace.

Ken whistled. "If all the traffic on this road is heading for the Pollard auction, it's going to be a pretty lively affair," he said.

Sandy nodded. "It must all be going there," he said. "This road is always completely deserted."

For five miles they crawled along, sometimes between high overgrown banks, sometimes between weed-choked ditches bordering fenced fields. Finally they turned into the lane leading off to the Pollard farmyard. Part way along it the truck they were following stopped, with its wheels deep in the dry dusty grass. Up ahead was a solid line of cars, already parked. Sandy guided Bert's car off the lane too, and parked behind the truck.

Before the boys stepped out on the road another vehicle was parked close to their rear bumper. The line of traffic behind them was as solid as the one they had followed.

Sandy reached for his camera case.

"Let's lock up," he said. "I wouldn't want Bert's car stolen out from under our noses."

Ken nodded vaguely. He was studying the people now leaving their cars, just behind and ahead of them, starting the walk to the house and barns at the end of the lane. One farmer in overalls had brought his whole family with him. The smaller children were chasing each other, kicking up clouds of dust. For that family, Ken suspected, the auction offered the chance of an outing. But other men, walking together in twos or threes, looked more serious. Ken felt sure they were already discussing among themselves the prices Pollard's larger pieces of equipment should bring.

"But why do you think those three men in the dark business suits—about fifty feet behind us, Sandy— are here today?" Ken asked, as he and Sandy joined the slowly moving parade. "They look as if the only garden they ever saw was on a penthouse roof."

Sandy threw a quick glance back at the men Ken indicated. All three of the faces had a city pallor, made more noticeable by dark sunglasses. Their clothes, too, set them apart from the rest of the crowd.

Sandy grinned. "I give up. Maybe it's becoming fashionable to use a tractor in penthouse flower boxes. Or maybe," he added more seriously, "they're in the real-estate business. Pop didn't seem to think Pollard was selling his land too, but maybe he is— and maybe those men are thinking of buying it and cutting it up into lots for a housing development."

"That's a possibility," Ken admitted, and made a mental note to check on whether the Pollard land was also on the market.

The boys separated as soon as they reached the end of the lane, and found themselves in the crowd milling around among the equipment that was about to go on the auction block. Ken noticed a couple of tractors, three farm trailers, a spray rig, and many more items, some of which he couldn't identify. Mr. Pollard was talking to the auctioneer, and Ken had to wait some time before he could get the farmer aside in order to question him.

Sandy was busy too. Ken saw him once, halfway up a towering maple, aiming his lens down at the whole crowded area between the Pollard house and the group of barns and sheds behind it.

About an hour and a half later, the boys joined forces again. The auction was just beginning to get under way. Sandy took another shot of Auctioneer Wilson in action, earnestly extolling the advantages of Pollard's spray rig, and then closed his camera.

"I've got everything I need," he said. "How about you?"

Ken nodded. "I guess so. I had a long talk with Pollard. He's getting out of farming because he says it's hard to make ends meet on a small farm these days. He says a farm has to be big—and fully mechanized to make it pay, and since he can't afford that kind of farm, he's giving up. But he's not selling his land now," Ken went on. "He thinks property values around here are going to zoom in the next ten years and he wants to hold on to his land until then. So he's going to rent his fields to the owner of a big farm down the road, and take a job in that farm-equipment center out on the highway."

"And Wilson?" Sandy asked. "Pop wanted you to talk to him too."

Ken nodded. "I did. And I arranged to phone him this evening and get a full account of the sale. So I'm ready to go if you—" He broke off as he caught sight of the three men in the dark business suits. They had been standing close to the boys. Now they moved off toward the parked cars, walking rapidly over the dusty earth. "I guess they discovered the land isn't for sale," he said.

"That's their problem," Sandy answered. "Give me time to pack my camera bag and then let's go."

A few minutes later they made their way back down the dusty lane and Ken got into the driver's

seat. The car wasn't as tightly wedged into its parking place as he had feared, and he managed to maneuver it out with only slight difficulty.

Now the road connecting Pollard's lane and the

highway was as deserted as Sandy had said it usually was. They covered half its length without seeing any traffic at all.

Ken slowed down for a sharp curve. A hundred feet on the far side of it a gray sedan was parked at the road's edge. He was almost abreast of the car before he saw the two men standing in front of it. One held a gallon can and had raised his arm to flag down the boys' car. Both wore dark glasses. Ken realized, as he braked to a stop some fifty feet beyond the parked vehicle, that the men were two of the three he had called to Sandy's attention earlier. The stran-

gers were having an unlucky day, he thought briefly, if they had come to the Pollard farm in the hope of buying it—and now found themselves without gas on their way home.

Sandy was already opening the door on his side as the car halted. "I'll go back and see what they want. Looks as if they need gas," he murmured. As he started back along the edge of the deep roadside ditch, he raised his voice. "Out of gas?"

"That's right." The man holding the gallon tin lifted it up. "We've got this, but it's empty." He and his companion started toward Sandy as he spoke. "So we thought if you could drive us to a gas station—"

"Sure," Sandy said. "Come along." He turned back toward Ken, still waiting in Bert's car. "We've got time to run them down to a gas station and back, haven't we, Ken?" he said, as the men approached. Without waiting for Ken's answer Sandy reached out to open the right-hand door of Bert's car, for the convenience of their newly acquired passengers. His hand was on the latch when one of the men, now some twenty feet behind him, spoke suddenly.

"Don't move! Stand right where you are!"

The violence in the harsh voice brought Sandy's head sharply around. Ken turned too, twisting in his seat.

One of the men still held the gallon tin. But now his companion held something, too.

In the man's right hand was a revolver, and its blunt barrel was aimed straight at Sandy!

CHAPTER III

SANDY SCENTS A LINK

Ken stared, his neck rigid in its twisted position, his eyes wide. One part of his mind told him that he must be dreaming—that the man pointing a gun at Sandy could not be real. Another part of his brain had absorbed the fact that the man holding the gun was as real as the gun itself, and that Sandy was in deadly danger.

Without turning to look, Ken knew that Sandy himself had not moved—that he stood frozen beside the car, his hand still outstretched toward the door handle, his gaze fixed on the weapon that threatened him with its round black eye.

Slowly the two men took one step toward Sandy, and then another.

"Don't move!" the man with the gun warned again. "Just stay right where you are!"

A voice inside Ken's head seemed to be screaming "Do something! Do something!"

For a split second Ken considered trying to reach

out, grab Sandy, haul him over the closed door into the car, and take off. The motor of the car was still running. He could be under way almost instantly.

But he knew it wouldn't work. He couldn't take the chance. Sandy had been ordered not to move, in a voice that meant business. And if Sandy did move— or was moved, by Ken—that gun might go off.

Suddenly Ken knew what he had to do. In the same instant he was acting on his knowledge.

Without turning forward in the seat, he flicked the gear selector into reverse and simultaneously jammed his foot down on the accelerator.

The wheels of Bert's car burned rubber with the suddenness of the surge of power. The car leaped rearward, charging back toward the oncoming men like an enraged animal.

Ken could see the jaws drop in the two pale faces. Each gaping mouth looked like a third dark circle beneath the two dark disks of the sunglasses above it.

For a second the men's bodies remained still, as frozen as Sandy's, left behind now at the spot where the car had been. Then the two men moved sideways. The man holding the gun collided with the other and lost his balance. The second man tottered. And suddenly they were both toppling into the ditch, arms flailing.

Ken saw the gallon tin arc through the air, just as he jammed on the brake, stopping the car as suddenly as if he had rammed it into a stone wall. He didn't know if the gun had flown wide too. He didn't wait to find out. He only knew that for a moment now the man who had held the gun was in no position to aim it.

Again Ken moved the gear selector and shifted his foot back to the accelerator. He would drive forward to where Sandy stood—

But Sandy was already moving toward the car. Then he was jerking open the door and tumbling into the seat beside Ken. Ken didn't give him a chance to shut the door. He shoved down hard on the accelerator and the car shot forward.

Ken kept his eye on the rear-view mirror. He saw the men in the ditch begin to haul themselves to their feet. He saw a hand with a gun in it raise itself and take aim at the car's wheels.

Then Sandy's hoarse cry pulled Ken's gaze back to the road in front of their racing car. Less than fifty feet ahead of them the narrow paving made one of its sharp turns. Ken managed to twist the steering wheel just in time to prevent the front tires from dipping into the ditch. Then they were around that curve and speeding toward the next one.

Sandy reached for the door and pulled it shut.

The fields and hedges on each side of them slid past in a blur. The speedometer needle jiggled frantically, as Ken braked for each twist in the road and then opened the throttle again beyond it.

At long last the highway came in sight. Ken swung

into the stream of traffic, saw a filling station several hundred yards away, and headed for it. When he had the car on the filling station pavement he pulled it far to one side and braked it to a halt. His hand shook as he fumbled for the ignition key and flicked it off.

"Whew!" he gasped, slumping down in the seat.

Slowly they turned and looked at each other. They were both breathing hard.

"What do you—think that—was all about?" Sandy gasped.

Ken shook his head slowly. His mouth was so dry that he had to swallow before he could speak. "I don't know," he said then. "And somehow it—didn't seem a good idea—to wait and find out."

"It sure didn't!" Sandy agreed fervently. "That was mighty quick thinking you did back there. I was petrified. That gun pointed at me so suddenly—" He broke off and ran a trembling hand over his damp forehead.

Ken turned to look back through the rear window, toward the intersection with the road they had just left.

"You think they'll follow us?" Sandy asked quickly.

"I haven't the faintest idea," Ken admitted. "I can't believe they'd do any gun waving out here on a crowded highway, anyway. But I'd like to see that car again just long enough to get the license number. I don't suppose you noticed it?"

"You suppose correctly," Sandy agreed grimly. "Ken," he added, as a sudden thought struck him, "those were two of the businessmen we were talking about earlier—do you remember? You noticed them right after we'd parked our car."

"I know," Ken said. "I recognized them too. They were the ones you said might be real-estate dealers. Only Pollard's land isn't for sale, and you'd think dealers might have found that out ahead of time, and saved themselves the trip. Besides, real-estate dealers don't make a practice of holding up people on the road."

"There were three of them when we saw them first," Sandy murmured. "I wonder what happened to the third one."

"Maybe he was posted along the road somewhere," Ken suggested, "to give the others a signal when a car was coming. So they could get out their prop— that empty gas can—and be all set to stage their holdup."

"You think that's what it was then?" Sandy asked. "An attempt at an ordinary holdup?"

"What else?" Ken eyed Sandy curiously. "Probably they figure a lot of the men at an auction have brought cash along, to pay for their purchases. For all we know our friends make a business of turning up at auctions, for that very reason."

"I suppose that's a possible explanation," Sandy said slowly. "But somehow I had the feeling that they weren't after money—that they were after *us*."

Ken stared at him. "What do you mean? You think they were planning to kidnap us?"

"It could be," Sandy said. "Don't forget that kind of thing has happened before. The reason you first came into the *Advance* office—remember that night? —was because you were looking for a place to hide. Somebody was after you then, because you were Dick Holt's son and they were getting at him through you. And down in south Jersey that time, when we landed in that kettle of fish Granger always calls *The Mystery of the Galloping Horse*—"

Ken's face had gone even paler under its tan. "I hadn't thought of that possibility," he said quietly.

"Well, think about it," Sandy said. "The easiest way to stop your father—if he's been investigating something that certain people don't want investigated— is to threaten your safety. Anyway, that's what a couple of people have thought once or twice before. So maybe that's what our friends think too."

"But—Granger said Dad had been at that trade conference and—" Ken spoke half to himself. "Yes, I guess a man like Dad could dig up something at an international trade conference that he thought needed investigation. And he wouldn't drop it just because—"

A figure was moving toward them from the direction of the gas pumps, and a politely curious voice called, "Anything I can do for you?"

The station attendant's commonplace question snapped the thread of their grim speculations.

"Er—no, thanks," Ken answered. "We were just sitting here for a minute trying to—er—decide what to do next."

"O.K." the attendant nodded, smiling, and turned to walk slowly back toward his row of pumps.

"Come on," Sandy muttered. "We can't stay here all day. Whoever those guys are, I think you're right about them—they won't follow us once we're out here on the highway. Let's get back to the office."

Ken turned the ignition key. "If that was an ordinary holdup attempt, we ought to report it to the police. If it wasn't—"

He didn't bother to finish the sentence. Sandy would know what he meant. The situation called for a conference with Bert and Pop.

In spite of their assurances to each other that they wouldn't be followed on the highway, Sandy kept glancing through the rear window all the way to Brentwood. They both sighed with relief when they stepped out of Bert's car behind the *Advance* office.

Their hands had stopped shaking. They were able to talk more coherently than they had earlier. They told their story in the fewest possible words.

Pop picked up the phone and put in a call to Granger the minute Sandy mentioned his own theory to explain what had just happened. The owner and editor of the *Advance* was scowling grimly around his pipe as he talked. "So what do you think, Granger?" he concluded. "Can Dick Holt be up to something that is causing alarm among certain elements on this side of the Atlantic? If the boys are going to be pawns in some game to shut Dick up, we want to know about it—and Dick will want to know too."

He listened in silence then for several moments.

"So what it amounts to is this: you just don't know, eh?" Pop said then. "Yes, I understand," he added. "So far as you're aware, Dick's not stepping on any crooked toes right now. But with him you never know. He could have involved himself in heaven-knows-what since you talked to him a couple of days ago."

Again he listened to Granger's voice on the other end of the wire. "All right," Pop said finally. "Let us hear from you if there's anything we should know. And in the meantime I'll see to it that the boys don't wander around on back-country roads for a while." He remembered then to thank Granger for the baseball tickets, and the two men spoke for a moment longer before Pop hung up.

"Well," Pop said, "we don't know any more than we did before." He pulled his glasses halfway down his nose and glared over them at the boys. "I'm going to ask Andy Kane to put a police guard on you two," he said, "unless you give me your solemn word you'll stay home at night for a while, stick to well-traveled roads in the daytime, and hightail it right back here or to the police if you see anything else that rouses your suspicions."

"We will, Pop," Ken assured him quickly. He knew from experience that a crusading journalist like his father could make ruthless enemies. For his father's sake, as well as for their own, Ken knew that he and Sandy had to keep out of the reach of such men. And he knew Sandy would be just as determined on that score as he was himself.

"Sure we will," Sandy agreed. "We don't have any desire to repeat today's experience, believe me." He shuddered. "I can still see that gun aiming right for here." He pointed to his chest. "If Ken hadn't thought and acted like lightning—" He shuddered again.

Pop had picked up the phone again and this time he called Andy Kane, his good friend and Brentwood's chief of police. Once more he related what had happened to the boys, but this time he gave additional details in order to supply the police with all possible information about the boys' assailants.

"No, they didn't get the license number," Pop said, in answer to one of Kane's questions. "Which is not surprising, I guess, under the circumstances. But they say it was a gray Buick—last year's model—four-door sedan. I'll put Ken on the phone and let him tell you anything more they remember about the men."

Ken took the phone. "Hello, Chief," he said.

"Hello, Ken," Kane said briskly. 'Sorry you boys had a nasty scare this morning. I'm hoping we can track those men down and put them out of circulation. What kind of a description can you give me?"

"Well," Ken said slowly, "all three of them—the two who stopped us and the one we'd seen with them earlier—were wearing hats and dark glasses, so we never did see the color of their eyes or hair. Let's see . . . the tallest one—he's the one we saw only once —must have been close to six feet and fairly thin. His clothes were dark, but I don't even remember what color they were. Do you, Sandy?"

Sandy shook his head.

"No, he doesn't either," Ken said into the phone. "But we can do a little better on the other two. The man who was holding the gasoline can was medium height—five nine or ten, I'd say—and medium build. His suit and hat were both dark gray. He wasn't quite as pale-faced as the other two. There was a little color in his cheeks. I'd imagine from his complexion that his eyes were blue and his hair light—or gray, maybe."

"Were they all old enough to have gray hair?" Kane wanted to know.

"They were middle-aged, I'd say—all of them," Ken told him. "They certainly weren't young, anyway. The third one—the one who held the gun on Sandy—was wearing brown. Brown hat, light-brown suit. Dark-brown tie, I think, and light shirt. And he was a lot stockier than his friend."

Again he glanced at Sandy.

Sandy shrugged. "I didn't like his expression," he said. "But I guess that wouldn't help the chief any. And maybe he wouldn't have looked the same to me if he hadn't had that gun in his hand." He shrugged again. "I guess that's all."

Then suddenly he snapped his fingers. "I've just thought of something! Here, give me the phone." He took it from Ken and spoke quickly into it. "Chief, I just remembered—when he shoved that gun toward me, and I was staring into it, I saw his cuff link. It was silver, I think—anyway, it looked like silver. And I guess I wouldn't have noticed it except that it made the gun look even more dangerous. Because it was in the shape of a scorpion—the cuff link, I mean."

Chief Kane made a noise somewhere between a snort and a laugh. "Nice observing, Sandy," he said. "But I can't believe it's going to do us much good. We can't very well haul in all the men in last year's Buick sedans and ask them to show us their cuff links."

"No, I suppose not," Sandy said. "But I bet there isn't another pair like that in the whole world. So if you ever do find a suspect, you can be sure he's our man if he's got a pair of cuff links like that."

"All right, Sandy. We'll keep it in mind." The chief

paused for a moment, as if glancing through his notes. "Well," he said finally, "we don't have too much to go on. All I can say now is that they don't seem to fit any descriptions that have come over our wire lately. And I never heard of any trio of middle-aged men pulling holdups around here. But we'll try. I'll circulate what you've given me. You never can tell. We might pick them up. Now let me speak to Ken again."

When the phone changed hands once more he said, "Listen, Ken, I remember a couple of spots of trouble you were in before this. I'll assign one of my men to you and Sandy if—"

"You won't have to do that," Ken said hastily. He knew how shorthanded Chief Kane always was. "We promised Pop we'll be very careful from now on, and we meant it. We shouldn't be in any danger walking around the streets of Brentwood in broad daylight, and that's what we plan to do for a while. Er—you won't mention all this to Mom, if you happen to see her, will you?"

There was a touch of amusement in Kane's voice when he answered. "I won't if you say so." He paused, and then added quickly, "If you see any of these characters around here let me know instantly."

They all felt a little easier once Chief Kane had been given the news. For a while longer Ken and the three Allens sat around discussing what had happened.

"Anyway," Sandy said finally, trying to strike a lighter note, "your car emerged safely from the crisis, Bert. You're just lucky we borrowed it today instead of yesterday." He shook his head. "You'd almost think we were being used as dummies in some kind of correspondence-school course in crime, wouldn't you? Yesterday someone attacks our car. Today someone attacks us. Tomorrow—?" He looked thoughtful for a moment. "Tomorrow," he said firmly, "I'm going to be very careful of my camera. I think that must be next on the list."

A few minutes later they left the office to pick up their car at Joe Meyers' garage. Bert offered to drive them over, on the way to an assignment.

"That's right," Sandy murmured. "You have to go and eat creamed chicken and peas."

"I've done that, thanks," Bert answered. "I'd just come back from the luncheon when you two came in."

"What!" Sandy's eyes went round. "You mean it's afternoon already—and I haven't had any lunch? Wow! I must have been even more scared than I knew, back there on that road."

"We'll go to the diner right opposite Joe's," Ken assured him, "as soon as we get the car."

"We sure will," Sandy said.

Bert, at the wheel, murmured, "I'd better get some gas at Joe's. Seems to me—" He took his eyes from the traffic for a quick glance at his gas gauge. "Well!" he said then. "Will wonders never cease! You mean to say you bought me a tankful of gas?"

"Of course you can pay us for it if you insist," his brother said.

"Oh, no," Bert said. "Have you forgotten that just a week ago I—"

"You don't have to," Sandy interrupted quickly. "I just said you could if you insisted on it."

They could all see the boys' red convertible standing to one side of Joe's lot as Bert pulled up.

"It's all ready for us," Ken said, opening the door and starting to get out. "Thanks, Bert."

"Remember," Bert said seriously, as Sandy joined Ken beside the car, "you really are going to be careful. Have a quick lunch and then go right back to the office. Pop'll be looking for you. Don't get any hare-brained ideas about going back to that road to look for clues to the identity of those thugs."

"Perish the thought," Sandy said solemnly. "If I don't drive on that road again for the rest of my life it will be all right with me."

"Good. Just stick to that mood of self-preservation," Bert said, and drove off with a wave.

The boys started toward their car. Joe Meyers hurried out of his garage to meet them.

"I was going to call you if you didn't come in soon," Joe said excitedly. "I wanted to give you the big news—for the *Advance*, you know."

"What news?" Ken asked.

"About the robbery—here—at my station! A robbery's big news, isn't it?" Joe asked. "Even if the thieves didn't get anything?"

Automatically Ken reached for the copy paper he always carried in his pocket. "Tell us about it, Joe. When did it happen?"

Joe didn't answer the question directly. He preferred to tell his story in his own way. "You know Tony Canzoni?" he asked.

The boys nodded. "You mean the policeman," Sandy said.

"That's right. Well," Joe told them, spacing his words for dramatic effect, "Tony was cruising by here about four this morning, and he sees these shadowy characters inside my office." He gestured toward the glass-fronted east end of his garage. "So Tony swings his car around fast, runs it in here, and goes to the garage to investigate. I guess the burglars saw his lights as they swept around, when he turned in the middle of the highway. Anyway, they take off before Tony gets to the garage. I figure they ran around the back of the station and jumped the fence into Mrs. Mason's back yard. Tony looks around for them but they're gone—poof! Like birds of the night, you might say. You can quote me on that," he added with a grin.

"I'll remember the phrase," Ken assured him. "But go on, Joe. You say they hadn't taken a thing?"

"That's right! There was a little money in the cash

register—and it was still there this morning. I was sure lucky. It must have happened the way Tony thinks—that he came by right after they'd broken in, and they took off before they had a chance to get their hands on anything."

"I guess you were lucky," Ken agreed. "I'm not even sure it's worth a story in the *Advance*," he added.

Joe Meyers reacted just as Ken had expected he would. "Oh, now listen! Why, they might have cleaned me out! And even if you don't want to run the story for my sake, you ought to do it for Tony. If he hadn't come by just then—"

"Don't worry, Joe," Sandy told him. "Ken was just trying to get a rise out of you. He'll write the story, all right."

"Good." Joe nodded with satisfaction. "My wife likes it when we get our name in the paper," he explained. "But mind you spell it right. Meyers, you know—with an 's.' Not Meyer."

"I know, Joe," Ken said.

They left a few minutes later, having stayed long enough to admire the job Joe had done on their car, and the new panel that now replaced the slit one in the convertible's top.

"Don't forget we'll need two separate bills," Ken reminded the garageman before they drove off. "The insurance company just gets billed for the top. We pay for the rest of the work ourselves."

"Don't worry," Joe promised with a grin. "I'll make sure you get your chance to help meet my overhead this month. You just remember to write a nice big story about my robbery."

"Lucky us," Ken remarked, as he waited for a chance to cross the highway toward the diner on the opposite side. "It's not every reporter who walks into a big ready-made front-page story like that, without any effort on his part."

Sandy didn't respond, but Ken scarcely noticed it. He and Sandy frequently made a point of pretending to ignore each other's attempts at humor.

But when Ken parked beside the diner, and got out of the car, he realized that Sandy was staring blankly through the windshield.

"Hey," Ken said. "We have arrived at the place where you can get food. Remember? F-O-O-D. That stuff you're so crazy about."

"Wait a minute, Ken," Sandy said, not shifting his gaze. "I'm thinking."

"And you'd rather think than eat?" Ken came close to the car. "You feeling all right?" he asked solicitously.

"I'm thinking about what you said a minute ago— about us walking into a ready-made story," Sandy said. " 'Lucky,' you said we were. And I think maybe you were wrong, Ken. I think—"

Ken leaned into the car. "Sandy," he said, "that was a joke. Get it? Not one of my best, I grant you.

But if I'd thought it was going to send you off the deep end, so that you even forgot you were hungry—"

"Listen, Ken," Sandy broke in. "We didn't walk into that story. It followed us. I mean, if we hadn't taken our car to Joe's garage yesterday, he wouldn't have had thieves in his place last night. We didn't walk into anything. We're *it*."

"Brother!" Ken said. "You need food more urgently than I thought! Haven't you noticed? Nobody stole our car out of Joe's garage. It's here. You're sitting in it. Come on—I'll personally buy you two large family-size hamburgers."

"I'm not being funny, Ken—or dazed from hunger either." Sandy turned and looked into Ken's face. "Just think for a minute. Put two and two together— or two and one, I should say. Yesterday somebody tried to steal our car—or anyway to break into it for some reason. This morning somebody tries to hold us up—or kidnap us or something. And in between those two events somebody breaks into Joe's garage while our car is there. Not before we take our car there. *While* it's there. See?"

Ken didn't reply for a moment. "No, I don't," he said finally. "I think it's about as farfetched a theory as I ever heard." Then he grinned. "But you know me. The more farfetched a theory is, the better I like it. Come on in the diner and let's talk it over."

Half an hour later they were back at the office, telling Pop about the various confusing possibilities that Sandy's theory had produced when they discussed it over their hamburgers.

"Hold on a minute," Pop said firmly. "Let's get a little order into this report. You're talking in circles."

"I know," Ken admitted. "But this thing goes in circles." He took a deep breath. "All right. We'll take the three things that have happened in the last twenty-four hours: somebody trying to get into our car, somebody breaking into Joe's garage last night while our car was there, and somebody—a couple of somebodies—holding Sandy and me up today. Sandy's idea is that there must be—well, that there could be, anyway—a common denominator in those three things."

Pop shook his head. "I don't see it. And, in any case, you two can't be the common denominator. You weren't in Joe's garage when it was robbed."

"But the car was," Sandy broke in.

"Neither can your car be the common denominator," Pop plowed on, disregarding the interruption, "because you weren't driving it when you were held up today." He thrust his pipe into his mouth, bit down hard on it for a moment and then took it out again.

"No," he said. "There is no one thing that ties everything together. The only logical explanation is that the first two events were regrettable, but perfectly ordinary attempts at robbery. That probably explains the third event too, but because of Dick Holt we must consider the possibility that these men wanted to kidnap you rather than rob you."

"But, Pop," Sandy said impatiently, "nobody with any sense would try to steal a car on the turnpike. Nobody with any sense would break into a car that's been emptied of everything that looks valuable. And if the men who robbed Joe last night were after money, they'd have headed for the cash register right after they broke in—fast enough to get at it even before Tony chased them. As for the men who held us up today"—Sandy shook his head—"they must be pretty dumb if they thought we were wealthy farmers carrying a lot of money to spend at the auction. How come there are so many stupid criminals buzzing around us all of a sudden?"

His father smiled at him wryly. "Why not, son? There are plenty of stupid criminals around, so why should you be surprised that those you happened to be involved with are among them." He leveled his pipe at Ken. "Except, of course, the holdup men today. They might be after you. And if so, they showed considerable cleverness in trailing you to the auction and in waylaying you on the way home. They're the ones I'm worried about. The others—" He shrugged. "There's nothing peculiar about them or about the way they blundered."

Sandy sighed. "You see?" he asked Ken. "You

heard my father. *He* doesn't think there's anything peculiar about his son being involved in three criminal events in less than twenty-four hours. *He* thinks it's perfectly natural that we should go around getting our car top slashed, and having our car in a garage that gets burgled, and being held up by guys who pulled a gun on us." He threw himself back in his chair. "With a father like that," he concluded, "it's a wonder I lived to my present ripe old age. It's a wonder I didn't die at the age of two months, the victim of—"

Sandy's voice died away. For a moment he was silent. Then suddenly he sprang to his feet. "I've got it!" he shouted. "I know what the common denominator is! My camera case! Somebody has made three separate attempts, within twenty-four hours, to get at my camera case! He—they—whoever they are— think there's something valuable in it. Maybe something planted by a criminal!"

"Now wait a minute!" his father said. "Why would a criminal—?"

"I can answer that!" Sandy interrupted. "When we were in the garage under the Global News building yesterday, the police were searching the place for a bank robber. So maybe the robber had been there —even if they never found him—and maybe he stashed millions of dollars' worth of bonds, or something, in the case of my camera. And ever since, after we got the loot safely out from under the eyes of the police for him, he's been trying to get them—it—back!"

"But, Sandy," Ken protested, "your camera case wasn't in the car when we left it at Joe's garage last night."

"But could the bank robber be sure of that?" Sandy demanded. "Of course he couldn't! But when he found it wasn't there, he had to try again. So that's why we were held up today! And whatever he put in my camera case must still be there—because those guys today never even got to first base with their attempt."

Sandy was heading for his darkroom as he spoke the last words. "I'll get my case," he shouted over his shoulder. "Probably whatever's hidden in it isn't something big like bonds. I'd have noticed anything that big. But it could be something small like diamonds or . . ." His voice faded away.

Sandy was back upstairs within seconds.

While Pop Allen and Ken watched, the redhead opened the canvas carryall that accompanied him on most assignments, and began to lay the objects it contained on his desk.

Pop, shaking his head once more, said, "I'd never have believed it—that you could get all those thingamajigs in one little bag."

Sandy was too busy to answer him. One by one, studying each before he put it down, he laid out half a dozen supplementary lenses, each in its own box, several extension cords, reflectors, film cartridges, flash bulbs, and various other items.

Finally he tipped the bag upside down, and tapped it gently. It was completely empty.

"Well," he said slowly, "I guess I haven't been carting around any stolen diamonds after all. But I still think there must be some common denominator to those three—"

"Sandy!" Ken interrupted him. "I've just thought of something. You mentioned a bank robber—"

"That's right," Sandy said. "The one the police were looking for in the Global News garage yesterday."

"But he hadn't robbed a bank," Ken said. "That's what I just remembered. The policeman we spoke to said it was an *attempted* bank robbery, not a—"

"You're right!" Sandy struck his forehead with a grimy palm in a gesture of despair. "And in that case—"

Bert, coming into the office just then, interrupted him. He was staring down at the assorted items spread on the surface of the desk.

"What kind of new game is this?" he asked.

"It's called," Pop told him, "Common Denominator, Common Denominator, who's got the Common Denominator? But I'm afraid you're too late to join in, Bert. I think even the brilliant inventors of this fascinating new pastime have given it up."

CHAPTER IV

BOOMERANG

Pop Allen was getting out of his car in the Allen driveway a little later, when the boys drove up behind him. Bert's car followed their red convertible. The smell of one of Mom's pot roasts came through an open kitchen window.

Pop waited for the boys outside the back door of the house. "Now remember," he said quietly, "you two are not leaving the house tonight. I think your common-denominator theory is a lot of nonsense. But until we get word from Granger that Dick Holt hasn't made some unpleasant enemies lately, I'm holding you to your word that you'll stay inside after dark."

"All right," Ken assured him. "We will. But what about that Boys Club meeting we were supposed to cover tonight? Mom knows we're supposed to be going to it. She's made some cookies or something for their refreshments, and she was saying yesterday we mustn't forget to take them along."

58

"Hmm," Pop said thoughtfully.

It was still understood among them that they wouldn't mention to Mom the fact that the boys had been held up, or tell her anything about the possible reason behind that event.

"Bert will have to go," Pop said.

"Where will Bert have to go?" Bert asked, coming up behind them. "Wherever it is, he can't go tonight. I've got a Zoning Board meeting to cover—remember?"

"That's right. So you have." Pop sighed. "Well, in that case, I'll have to take care of the Boys Club myself. Mom was counting on me to go along with her to see her sister, but she'll understand. After all these years she knows enough not to be surprised by an unexpected assignment."

"But how'll we explain the fact that we're not going ourselves?" Sandy asked.

The telephone bell sounded inside the house. The quick cutting-off of the ring told them that Mom had answered it.

"Leave it to me," Pop said. "I'll figure out something. I'll tell her that—"

"Ken! Are you out there?" Mom's voice called through the open window. "Oh, good!" she hurried on. "I thought I'd heard the cars. Ken, hurry up! Your father's on the phone!"

Ken took the three steps to the kitchen porch in one leap. "Thanks, Mom!" he shouted, on his way through the kitchen to the telephone in the hall. Eagerly he grabbed the receiver. "Dad! Hello!"

"Hello, Ken," his father's familiar voice said over the wire. "How are you?"

"Fine," Ken assured him. "And so's the rest of the family. Where are you? Granger said you were heading for Algiers."

"I was," Dick Holt said. "And that's where I am. Got in half an hour ago and found Granger had put in a call for me here. I've just talked to him."

"Oh!" Ken said. "Then he told you—"

"He told me the whole story, Ken," Dick Holt interrupted. "And I assured him that I haven't stuck my finger into any kind of a hornets' nest for several months. So that little incident today can't have been engineered by anybody who was trying to injure me through you."

"That's great!" His father's words lifted a weight from Ken's mind. That meant that no danger threatened either Dick Holt, or Sandy and himself. 'That's great!" Ken repeated, grinning.

Pop Allen had come to stand in the doorway to the hall. Ken glanced up at him. "It's all right, Pop," he said quietly.

"But, Ken," Dick Holt was saying, "I don't like this business of you and Sandy being held up. What's happening around Brentwood? You having a crime wave there?"

"No, of course not." Ken laughed. "Nothing like that has happened around here in ages—and probably won't again." He lowered his voice, hoping Mom wasn't overhearing. "The men obviously came out from the city. There was this big auction, you see, and they probably thought—"

"I know," Dick Holt would understand why Ken was speaking quietly. "Granger told me the setup. But I should think you might have guessed what they were up to, Ken. Pretending to be out of gas— why that trick is so old it's got moss on it."

"And of course you've brought me up never to stop and offer help to anybody who seems to be in trouble," Ken told him, grinning into the phone.

"Of course I've done nothing of the kind!" his father said. "All right, Ken. I didn't mean to jump on you. But it worries me when I hear of you being in danger when I'm halfway around the world and can't do anything about it."

"You couldn't have done anything if you were here," Ken reminded him. "It was all over in about thirty seconds. And now that we know there's no reason to think it might happen again—or anything like it—we'll forget the whole business. Now let's talk about something interesting. When are you coming home?"

"I told Mom about that," Dick Holt said. "I told her that was my reason for calling."

Ken grinned to himself. His father too had long been a member of the conspiracy to keep Mom from worrying unnecessarily.

"I'm planning to land in New York a week from Friday," Dick Holt was explaining, "just as I'd told Granger before. So I'll be on hand for Pop's birthday. What are you boys getting him?"

"Well—er—"

"I see. He's right there and you can't talk. All right. I'll just have to take a chance on not duplicating whatever you've bought. Let me talk to Pop, will you, Ken? I want to tell him myself that that possibility you've been worrying about just isn't in the cards." Then Holt added quickly, "But wait. Give Bert and Sandy my best. And take care of yourself now—you hear?"

"Yes, sir. I hear. And the same to you. It'll be great to see you, Dad. I'll put Pop on. Good-by!"

"Good-by, Ken—until next week."

Ken handed Pop the phone and went out into the kitchen, where Mom hurried over, reached up to pull down his head, and kissed him.

"That's because I'm so pleased!" she announced. "Isn't it wonderful—to think that Dick will be here in just a little over a week? I'll start getting his room ready tomorrow morning. I think I'll take the curtains down and wash them."

"That's what Dick Holt comes here for, Mom—to sleep in a room with nice clean curtains," Bert said, laughing. But he and Sandy were eying Ken sharply. And as soon as their mother turned back to the stove they raised their eyebrows at him questioningly.

"Yes," Ken said. "It's all right." A nod of his head told them he was answering their unspoken question. "I mean," he hurried on, "Dad really is going to get home on schedule for once. Yes, sir, it's all right!"

When Pop came into the kitchen a few moments later, his own conversation with Dick Holt at an end, the smile on his face matched the grins that greeted him.

"Why isn't supper ready, Mom?" he demanded. "How do you expect me to take you over to your sister's tonight, if we're not going to sit down to the table until midnight or thereabouts?"

"What a way to talk!" Mrs. Allen scolded him. "We're ready to sit down right this minute. My goodness!" she went on, as she transferred the pot roast from its pan to a platter, "what a fine evening! First the call from Dick—and now you say you're free tonight, Albert. I was afraid something important would come up that would mean you'd have to work after all."

"No," Pop said blandly. "There's not a thing. I thought for a little while there I might have to cover a meeting, but it turns out I was wrong. Didn't I hear the boys say they were taking some of your cookies to that Boys Club meeting tonight? Or did you forget to bake them?"

"Of course I didn't forget," Mon answered briskly. "I've got them all ready. They're in that box there by the door."

Sandy eyed it. "It looks pretty heavy," he said. "I may have to eat a few before we leave, so we won't strain our backs getting it out to the car."

"You'll do no such a thing!" his mother told him, sounding shocked.

They all laughed at her. And all during the meal together they found things to laugh at. Mom said once, beaming at them, that they seemed in unusually fine spirits.

"It's because of Dick's call, I know," she added, giving Ken a special smile.

"That's right, Mom," Pop assured her. "Why shouldn't we all feel great—to know that Dick will be here soon?"

David Tanner, the *Advance* printer and a Boys Club adviser, who usually rode to the meeting with Ken and Sandy, found them all still at the table when he arrived. "What's up?" he asked. "You look like a party."

Mom answered him. "We feel like a party. Ken's father will be home next week!"

Tanner accepted her explanation of their mood, and nobody added that Pop and Bert and the boys had an additional reason for feeling jubilant that evening.

The Boys Club meeting was over shortly before

ten, and Tanner went to the *Advance* office with Ken and Sandy, to check over his work for the next day. Sandy disappeared immediately into his basement darkroom, to develop the pictures he had taken during the day. Ken telephoned Wilson, the auctioneer, obtained the information he needed from him, and settled down to work at his typewriter.

Bert came in a quarter of an hour later, just as Tanner was leaving, and began to rattle the keys of his own machine. By eleven o'clock they were all finished with the work they had set themselves, and ready to go home.

"I'll buy you pie and coffee first," Bert offered.

"We accept," Sandy said quickly. "Come on. Let's go over to the diner on the highway right away, before your generous impulse dies."

"I forgot to ask you, Sandy," Ken said a little later, looking across the table of the booth they occupied. "Did your pictures of the auction turn out all right?"

Bert, alongside his brother, spoke before Sandy had a chance to answer. "Did he ever take pictures that he didn't think were magnificent? Come on, Sandy," he prodded, "tell us why the ones you took today are probably the finest shots made since the invention of the camera."

Sandy didn't answer. His fork was in mid-air, his gaze fixed intently on the far end of the narrow room, with its counter and its single row of booths.

"If you're gazing wistfully at the sandwiches," Ken told him, "Bert's offer didn't include—"

Sandy interrupted him. "Ken," he said quietly, "turn around—sort of casual, like—and take a look at the man sitting at the counter, five stools down."

Ken glanced briefly at his friend, saw the intent look on his face, and obeyed.

When he turned back again he took a swallow of coffee before he spoke. "I know what you mean," he said. "But I can't be sure. You think that's the guy who held a gun on you today."

"Huh?" Bert too had instinctively looked at the man Sandy mentioned. Now he looked again.

None of them spoke for a moment.

Then Bert said soberly, "If you really think that's the man, we'd better call Kane.

"I know," Ken said. "If I could see him full face, I'm pretty sure I'd know, one way or the other. But as it is, just seeing his profile—"

"That's it," Sandy muttered. "I wish he'd turn around. Do you think one of us could risk walking down there, Bert?"

"Then he'd probably see you too," Bert pointed out. "And if he recognized you, and knew you could turn him over to the police, he wouldn't be likely to hang around until—" Bert broke off abruptly. "I'll be jiggered!" he said softly. "Sandy! Quick! Watch his arm when he reaches out again to put the sugar back!"

"Take a look at that man," Sandy whispered

Ken, not daring to turn around again, could only stare at the faces of his two friends across the table. He saw Sandy's eyes go wide, his jaw tighten.

"A silver scorpion cuff link!" Sandy breathed.

"What?" Ken said. "Are you sure?"

"I saw it myself," Bert assured him. "I thought maybe I was dreaming the first time. I didn't even take Sandy seriously this afternoon when he told Kane about it. But I saw it, Ken! And now that Sandy's seen it too—!"

"I saw it all right," Sandy said. "And I'd know it anywhere. Let's call Kane—fast!" He half rose from his seat.

Bert's hand restrained him. "The phone booth's down at the other end of the diner. You'd have to pass him to get there. So let me do it. You two stay here and don't call attention to yourselves. Keep your head down, Sandy. If he looks over this way you don't want him to see you staring. It'll take Kane a couple of minutes to get down here. We don't want to scare the quarry off before he arrives."

"All right," Sandy muttered. "But tell Chief Kane to hurry it up."

Bert got up and moved along the aisle toward the telephone booth. He seemed intent on his goal. He didn't look at the counter customers as he walked past them.

"I hope old Scorpion Cuff Link is still carrying that gun," Sandy muttered into his coffee cup. "Having

a concealed weapon on his person will be enough
to put him out of circulation for a while. It's going to
give me real pleasure to put the finger on that guy.
For two cents I'd go down there right now and put
five fingers on him—all curled up in a fist!"

His voice had risen slightly on the last words.

"Sandy!" Ken said warningly. "Keep it down." He
flagged a waiter and asked for their check.

While the man stood beside them, totaling up the
bill, Sandy took a sip of coffee and another bite of
pie. But as soon as the waiter moved away Sandy
said, "What's taking Bert so long?"

"Relax," Ken advised. "He's only been gone a
couple of minutes." He was putting money on the
table for a tip.

The big hand of the electric clock on the diner wall
rolled off another minute, and then one more. Ken
took his last swallow of cold coffee. Sandy finished
his pie and laid the fork on the plate. Then his eyes
went to the phone booth.

"Still talking!" he muttered. "The first thing you
know our friend will walk out of here and— He's
getting up, Ken! He's leaving now!" He put his hands
on the table top to push himself up.

"Stay where you are!" Ken said. "He has to stop at
the cashier's desk to pay his check."

"He's paid it already," Sandy said an instant later.
"Come on! We've got to follow him."

"We've got to get his car license, anyway," Ken

agreed. "But give him a chance to get outside, so he doesn't see us coming after him."

"All right! Let's go!" Sandy said. "He's through the door already. You get Bert out of the phone booth and join me outside."

They walked down the aisle together. Ken put money and their bill on the cashier's desk as he went past. Sandy swung toward the outer door. Ken continued toward the phone booth.

He pushed open the door of the booth. "Quick!" he said. "He's gone! Sandy's outside trying—"

Bert didn't wait for him to finish. "He's gone outside, Andy," he said into the mouthpiece. "We'll try to get his license number and a description of his car at least, if he drives off before . . . No, we won't tangle with him. We'll wait for you here."

Swiftly he hung up the phone and he and Ken walked together through the outer door. Sandy was standing just beyond it, in a patch of shadow.

Most of the big semicircular parking area between the diner and the highway was brightly floodlighted, and there were big lights over the entrance and exit driveways.

"He's heading down that way—see?" Sandy said swiftly. "His car must be parked down there near the exit—close to where ours is parked."

A large truck and trailer, extending from the highway's edge far into the parking lot, cut off their view of the exit end of the lot.

"But if he gets around the far side of that trailer, we won't be able to see what car he gets into—unless we're right behind him," Sandy went on. "Come on!"

Bert held them back a moment. "If he turns around he'll see us coming toward him," he said. "This light is so bright— All right, let's go now," he added, as the man rounded the end of the big trailer and disappeared from their sight.

With long strides they covered the floodlighted area, aiming for the huge trailer.

When they reached the near side of it they paused for a moment.

"I don't hear an engine starting," Sandy muttered. "But with the traffic noises on the highway—"

"Let's go this way," Ken suggested, moving along the near side of the trailer truck toward its rear.

They edged around the back of the truck into the area it shadowed. Even the light over the driveway exit was cut off there by another big trailer parked parallel to the highway, forming a right angle with the huge vehicle around which they had just detoured. Within the angle formed by the two trucks stood four cars, parked parallel to each other, their rear ends toward the trailer that stood like a wall between them and the highway.

One of the cars was the boys' convertible. On one side of it was a medium-sized closed truck. On the other side was a low-slung sports car and another smaller truck. There was no sign of the Buick sedan the boys had seen that morning. There was no sign of the man they had followed.

"We've lost him!" Sandy muttered under his breath.

"Maybe his car's parked somewhere out on the highway," Bert suggested quietly. "Let's go look."

They started along the narrow aisle formed by the big truck and the rear ends of the four smaller vehicles, including their own. Sandy was in the lead, moving at a rapid pace. Ken and Bert were right behind him.

They were passing the rear of their own car when a figure popped out into the aisle like a jack-in-the-box, from the narrow space between the convertible and the sports car beyond it. Even in the shadow the man was recognizable as the one they had been following. Even in the shadow it was obvious that the bulge in his outthrust coat pocket had the shape of a gun.

"That's far enough!" the man said, blocking Sandy's path. "Stop right where you are!"

For an instant Bert and the two boys stood frozen in their tracks. Then Ken swung around, in the wild hope that Andy Kane was even at that moment driving into the parking area entrance. If he could get around the big trailer—

"Don't try anything!" A second voice spoke the command. And in the same instant the second figure

appeared, stepping out from between the convertible
and the closed truck. When Ken had seen him last the
man had been tumbling into a ditch, flinging wide
the empty gasoline can he had held.

"No noise—no sudden moves," the first man continued. "You're covered from both directions. And
this time you're not going to get away!"

CHAPTER V

HELPLESS

THE suddenness of their capture had a paralyzing effect. Ken stared blankly into the muzzle of the second man's gun, telling himself that nobody would seriously attempt a holdup within yards of a busy highway, within a few hundred feet of a busy diner crowded with people.

Then his mind started to function again, and he knew that Bert and Sandy and he were trapped as effectively as if they had been surrounded by enemies in the wilds of a jungle.

"What do you think you're doing?" It was Bert's voice that asked the question, and it crackled with anger.

Ken swung around so that, like Bert and Sandy, he faced the man with the scorpion cuff links.

"Just keep quiet, bud, and everything will be all right." The metal insect on the man's left wrist winked in a gleam of light as he gestured Bert and the boys toward the dark space between their convertible and the closed truck parked beside it. "Come on, Chet," he added. "Let's get them into the truck."

"I'm not going to keep quiet and let you—" Bert began again. A sudden gasp cut off his words.

"That's right." The man called Chet sounded amused. "That's a gun poking into your spine, bud. And don't think I'd be afraid to use it. There's plenty of traffic noises around here to cover up a shot."

"Take it easy, Bert," Ken said quickly. He knew this was no time to risk a bullet. Andy Kane was already on his way. What they had to do was stall their captors, and get them out from behind the protection of the parked cars so that the chief of police could see them the moment he drove up.

"There's some mistake here," Ken hurried on, addressing himself to Bert. "These men have apparently confused us with somebody else. Look," he said to the man with the scorpion cuff links, "we don't know who you think we are. But if you'll just walk out there into the light with us, and take a good look, you'll see—"

"You shut up too, bud!"

Now Ken gasped at the painful jab of a gun muzzle in his back.

"Just listen for a minute instead of talking," the man called Chet went on. "We know who you are, all right. And we know you've got it. But if you want to hand it over right now, we may not have to—"

" 'Got it!' " Sandy broke in explosively. "What do you mean—we've 'got it'? What are you talking about?"

"Did you hear that, Dan?" Chet said. "They're going to play it dumb."

"I heard it." Again a gleam of light caught the silver scorpion on the wrist of the man who had been addressed as Dan. "Well, that's what we expected." He raised his voice slightly. "All right, Vic. Open the truck door."

A grating sound at the boys' back told them that the order had been carried out.

"Turn around now, all three of you," Dan commanded. "I said turn!" he snapped, as they continued to stand motionless facing him.

Slowly, reluctantly, they did as they had been told.

Once they had been herded inside the truck, Ken knew, Andy Kane would never see them. "We're not trying to play dumb," he said desperately. "We don't know what you're talking about. And that's the truth. Unless—" A sudden thought struck him and he thought it might at least give them another precious second or two. "Did you hide something in my friend's camera case?" he asked.

"In his camera case?" Now, for an instant, it was Dan who seemed to be confused.

"Yes. Did you?" Sandy hastily seized the chance Ken had given them to stall a little longer. "Because if you did, it's not there any more. I mean, I emptied out my case yesterday and—"

"Who said anything about a camera case?" Chet growled. He had moved slightly to stand beside the truck, which the boys were now facing. They could see that a door in its side was open, and that a shadowy figure stood just inside it. "Go on—climb up into the truck," Chet went on. "You first." He gestured toward Ken.

"Get their car keys from him," Dan said. "He's got them—he's the one who was driving."

"Right. Hand them over," Chet ordered.

Ken reached first into his left pocket, and pulled his hand out empty. "No," he muttered. "I guess they're—" As slowly as he dared he reached into his right pocket. Every second gained gave Kane that much more chance to arrive in time.

"Hurry it up!" Chet told him.

"But if you say you didn't put anything in my camera case—" Sandy began again.

"Yes!" Bert picked it up. "If you'd just tell us what it is you think we've got—"

Dan interrupted him. "Chet, if Black Hair hasn't found those car keys yet, maybe a little persuasion—"

"Here they are." Grimly Ken handed them over.

"All right. In with you now." Chet punctuated his order with another jab of his gun.

Under its pressure Ken moved helplessly toward the open door in the side of the truck. As a last resort he raised his voice, in the futile hope that Andy Kane, perhaps somewhere in the parking area now, would hear him. "You're making a mistake, you know. We—"

"Quiet!" Chet thrust him forcefully forward.

Ken stumbled. His head struck against the metal side of the truck. Dazed by the blow he felt himself being hauled up through the open doorway by strong hands that grasped his shoulders. The same hands shoved him toward the forward end of the truck's interior.

"Sit down!" a new voice snapped.

Ken did as he was told, slumping onto the dusty floor and leaning back against the panel that separated the truck body from the driver's cab.

The man inside the truck with him, the man Dan had called Vic, was silhouetted by the light mounted on the rear wall of the truck. His lean height told Ken that he was the third man in the group he and Sandy had seen the day before, at the auction.

Since this morning, the three men had apparently been following Sandy and himself. But why? Ken wondered frantically. What was it the men thought they had?

As the questions spun around in his throbbing head Bert appeared in the doorway and was brusquely ordered to sit on Ken's right. A moment later Vic's long thin arm, with a gun at the end of it, prodded Sandy to a seat on Ken's left.

Surely Andy Kane had arrived by now, Ken told himself.

But what could the chief do? He would be searching the parking area for Bert and the boys, and for a Buick sedan. He would have no idea— But Kane would recognize the red convertible, Ken thought suddenly. And if he came close to it—!

"Why don't you search us?" Ken asked loudly. "If you think we've got something that belongs to you—"

"Keep your voice down!" Vic commanded coldly. The tall, thin man was already beginning to slide shut the door in the side of the truck. When he spoke again he directed his voice through the remaining slit. "O.K., Dan," he said. "We're all set in here. Lock the door and let's get moving. Chet's going to follow us with their car, isn't he?"

"Right." Dan spoke the one word quietly. Then he pulled the door tight, and Ken could hear the snap of a lock.

Sandy broke the dead black silence. "You ought to search us," he said. "That would prove to you—"

Vic cut him off. "A search would prove nothing. We know you haven't got it on you."

As he spoke the truck's engine rumbled into life. Ken could see that Vic had taken up a position in the right-rear corner. Feet planted wide, back braced against the truck walls, he stood with his arms crossed and his gun pointed right at Ken.

"Let's get one thing straight," Vic said. "Anybody

here makes one move toward me—and Black Hair there in the middle gets it. Is that clear?"

The truck lurched forward, and Ken swayed as it swung in a tight curve toward the exit that led onto the highway.

Ken's fists clenched in helpless anger. A moment's thought had told him that Andy Kane could not possibly have arrived at the diner in time to see their red convertible driving off behind a truck. In spite of their desperate efforts to stall, less than two minutes must have elapsed from the time they encountered the armed men until the moment the truck—with the convertible behind it—left the parking area.

Ken had no doubt that the entire Brentwood police force would be looking for them very soon. But he knew now that their captors would almost certainly get the convertible out of sight very quickly. And Andy Kane would have no reason to be suspicious of any truck he or his men might see. He would be looking for the Buick sedan Ken and Sandy had mentioned to him.

Ken's anger changed to despair when he looked once more at the coldly efficient man who was guarding them. There would be no chance of taking him by surprise. He was far too alert, far too intent on his job. And he knew his business. He had bunched Ken and the two Allens in a tight group, so that from his vantage point at the other end of the truck he could keep all of them under constant watch.

Ken glanced sideways, first at Sandy and then at Bert. Sandy seemed almost relaxed, knees drawn up and arms wrapped around them, swaying with the jouncing of the truck. But Ken had been in tough spots with Sandy before. He knew that the redhead was as tense as himself, waiting for an unmistakable opportunity for action, or for some lead from Ken himself. Then, in an instant, that deceptively relaxed appearance could explode into powerful activity.

Bert was a more dubious quantity. Jaw clenched, back upright, he sat rigid with his hands pressed against the floor, as if at any moment he might launch himself forward in an attack on their guard.

"Don't try anything!" Ken begged him. He barely breathed the words out of the side of his mouth, so that they would not be audible above the sound of the engine. He couldn't be sure Bert had even heard him.

He only hoped Bert would realize, as he did himself, that all they could do at the moment was to wait—and perhaps to find out a little more about the reason behind their mysterious capture.

Ken cleared his throat loudly. "What makes you so sure we have—whatever it is you're looking for?" he asked.

"Still playing it dumb, eh?" Vic smiled briefly, but his gun didn't shift its aim.

Bert's body leaned slightly forward. "That's the only way we can play it!" he snapped. "How many times do we have to tell you that we haven't the slightest idea of what you're talking about?"

"You'd be surprised how fast dumb people sometimes smarten up," the man said, ignoring Bert. "All they need is a little persuasion."

Bert's body leaned another fraction of an inch forward. Ken spoke hastily, to forestall a more reckless move on Bert's part, "Maybe we'd smarten up if you'd give us a little information," hoping the words sounded more reasonable than he felt. "We really don't even know how we're supposed to have acquired this thing you're looking for. And we certainly don't know what it is."

The truck swerved at that moment, and Ken knew it had turned off the highway onto a side road. His heart sank. If the convertible had left the highway too, Chief Kane and his men would have more trouble spotting it.

How far had they come from the diner? Ken wondered. Not very far, he knew.

Absorbed in his thoughts he almost failed to realize that the man with the gun was actually giving them some of the information Ken had sought.

"What it is is none of your business," Vic was saying. "But how you got it—" He laughed. "You got it when we put it in your car, of course. And if you'd let me get it out again—when you stopped at that turnpike restaurant yesterday afternoon—you wouldn't be in this spot now. You've been asking for it, trying to be so smart."

Sandy caught his breath. "Asking for it!"

"But why our car?" Ken asked quickly. "And where in the car—?"

"That's enough," the man broke in flatly. "I'm just a hired hand. It's not my business to answer your questions. But I'll give you a little advice," he added a moment later. "If you'll be really smart for a change, and give the boss what he's after, you'll come out of this with whole skins and maybe even with a little something for your trouble. The boss is a generous man, see?"

"If your boss is responsible for us being—" Bert began.

"Save it!" Vic snapped. "It's not my business to listen to your complaints, either."

Once more the truck swerved, and this time it bounced off the paved road. Its wheels began to jounce as they rolled into holes and out of them again.

How long, Ken wondered, would it take Chief Kane and his men to search every unpaved lane in the country surrounding Brentwood?

"I'll just give you one more piece of advice," Vic was saying. He had flattened one hand against the back of the truck, to steady himself against the uneven motion of the floor beneath his feet. "My buddies," Vic went on, "are just waiting for a chance to get to work on you two. They didn't like what you did to them this morning, running your car at them and dumping them into that ditch. And they didn't like what the boss said to them when they came back without the—well, when they came back. He gave them a rough going over. And they'd be glad to give you one too, believe me—and not just with words, either. So watch your step, see?"

A moment later the truck's brakes went on again, and then once more it swerved. Almost instantly the engine began to labor, as if the vehicle were climbing a steep grade. The jouncing grew worse.

Ken felt himself toppling to the left, and he braced himself with a hand against the floor. Instantly he realized that the man standing at the far end of the truck was also having trouble maintaining his balance. It would be a good time to jump him—to—

But the thought had barely formulated itself in Ken's mind when the truck brakes went on once more and the vehicle ground to a halt.

The panel in the wall above Ken's head slid open.

"O.K. back there?" The voice that spoke from the driver's seat belonged to the man who wore scorpion cuff links.

"Sure," Vic assured him. "We there already?"

"This is where we're putting on the blindfolds. Chet's coming up right behind us. He'll help you." As Dan spoke he turned around to kneel on the seat of the cab, so that he was looking directly down on Bert and the boys.

Ken glanced upward and saw the gun in the man's hand. Faintly he could hear another car stop nearby. Then the lock on the sliding door of the truck body rattled, and the door slid open. Chet climbed in, tossing several white cloths in ahead of him. Once inside, he slid the door shut again.

Dan took command, as he had earlier. "You!" He reached down and touched Bert on the shoulder. "Get up and move out into the middle of the truck. Stand with your back toward me. All right, Chet. Go ahead and fix him up."

While Bert stood helpless, between Dan's gun at one end of the truck and Vic's at the other, Chet carried out an assignment that had obviously been well planned ahead of time.

"Put your hands behind your back," Chet ordered. "And cross your wrists." When Bert obeyed, Chet bound the wrists tightly with wide strips of adhesive tape torn from a roll taken from his pocket. Then he took one of the cloths—it looked like a towel, Ken thought—folded it in thirds, and put it over Bert's eyes. He tied the ends firmly behind Bert's head. Then he ran his hands lightly over Bert, patting his pockets in a quick search for weapons.

"Lead him back to his place, Chet," Dan ordered, and Chet conducted the blinded Bert back to the corner. "Sit down again," Dan told Bert.

Ken looked on in helpless sympathy while Bert lowered himself to his knees, and then slumped sideways into a sitting position, arms awkwardly stiff behind him, legs straightened forward on the floor.

"You next." Dan's hand touched Sandy's shoulder, and Chet hauled the redhead to his feet and pulled him toward the middle of the truck.

Again Ken watched while his friend's wrists and eyes were bound, and his pockets tapped.

When Sandy had been returned to his place, it was Ken's turn.

He did his best to hold his wrists slightly apart, to earn himself some leeway in the tape binding. But his captor was too smart for the success of that trick. The man called Chet pulled hard enough to jam Ken's wrists painfully together under four or five bracelets of taut adhesive. Then a folded towel was wrapped around Ken's head and knotted. Ken's wrists and head were both throbbing by the time he had been led back to his position against the wall, and told to sit down once more.

These men were experts, Ken admitted grimly to himself. Their bindings would leave no permanent marks. But Sandy, Bert, and he were effectively prevented from seeing where they would be taken from now on. And when they encountered the "boss" Vic had spoken of, they would not see his face.

A cold chill ran down Ken's spine as he realized the probable significance of the elaborate precautions being taken by the "boss's" men. They must mean that the "boss" himself was a well-known criminal—a man whose past forced him to go to extreme lengths to avoid identification.

Footsteps and the banging of the door told Ken that Chet had left the truck.

"Ready?" Dan's voice asked.

"Ready," Vic replied.

Then the truck's engine came to life again, and whined in low gear as the vehicle moved slowly forward once more. This time it traveled for only a few minutes before it swerved left and jolted to a final stop.

The door slid open. Ken felt the rush of cool night air against his cheek, and heard the loud sounds of a summer night's insects.

Then he heard other sounds—men's voices that grew gradually louder until he could identify two separate speakers. One spoke hoarsely, the other in a soft low-pitched voice.

"Well, I see you got them!" The hoarse voice was suddenly so close that Ken knew the man must be peering through the open door of the truck. "What kept you—?" The words stopped short and for an instant there was silence. Then the voice demanded, "What's this? Who's the third joker?"

Dan answered from directly above Ken's head. "We couldn't help it, boss." Dan was no longer a ringleader who issued commands. He sounded apologetic, almost frightened. "He was with them. We had to take him along."

"Can't you do anything right?" The voice was even harsher now that anger was roughening it.

"But it wasn't our fault, boss," Chet said hurriedly. "There was somebody with them all evening. We never had a chance to pick them up alone."

"What difference does it make, Frank?" the smooth voice asked soothingly. "I'm sure we'll find that they'll be co-operative, and in that case we'll be sending them all on their way home very shortly. So it doesn't really matter whether there are two of them, or three."

"Maybe." The hoarse voice didn't seem convinced. Then, in an attempt at a whisper, it added, "No names! Didn't I tell you? Not even first names!"

There was a note of amusement in the smooth voice when it answered. "But we're Frank and Earnest, Frank! Isn't that safe enough?"

"Huh? Oh, I get it. Frank and Earnest—yeah, that's good. Sure, that's who we are. All right, Earnest," the voice added, "let's get going here. We've wasted enough time!"

Ken thought of his joke in Granger's office, when he had introduced Sandy and himself as Riff and Raff. Had that been only yesterday? It seemed years go.

"Just let me talk to them a minute, Frank," the man who had called himself Earnest said. "Our guests have probably been seriously frightened. I want to assure them that no harm will come to them."

A scraping noise suggested that the man had climbed into the truck. When he spoke again it was clear that he was standing within a few feet of Ken.

"There's nothing for you to worry about," he said. "Nothing at all. You probably don't believe me. I confess I'd be somewhat skeptical myself, in your position. But we were forced to take this rather—er —unorthodox method of meeting with you, owing to certain circumstances which I needn't go into. Now all we want from you is something that actually belongs to us—something I know you'll be glad to turn over to us without any argument. We put it in your car for temporary safekeeping, and now we want it back. That's all there is to it. You see? As soon as it's in our hands again, you three will be free to go."

"That's right." The man with the hoarse voice was obviously attempting to sound genial. "It's just the way he told you. In fact it's better than that. I understand one of my men here caused a little damage to your car. And we've kept you up kind of late, bringing you out here. So I've got a couple of hundred bucks here in my pocket that'll be turned over to you when you leave. We couldn't be fairer than that— now could we? So you just tell us where our property is."

"We don't even know what you're talking about," Ken said evenly. "We've already told your men that.

If you put something in our car, we didn't know it. And we don't know where it is now."

"Listen, you—!" Frank began roughly.

"Wait, Frank," the other man said, still speaking quietly. "Perhaps they still don't understand. This thing that belongs to us," he went on, "is of no value to you whatsoever. It is simply an envelope—a brown envelope measuring about nine by twelve inches."

"They know what it is all right!" Frank said. "They've been hiding it, haven't they? You're wasting time."

"Perhaps they didn't know," the smooth voice persisted. His voice had taken on a new quality, and Ken sensed that the man had leaned over them with a confidential air. "I'm giving you the full benefit of the doubt, you see," he said. "I'm willing to believe that you found this envelope, didn't realize it wasn't yours, and simply put it away somewhere—perhaps absent-mindedly." He made the ridiculous suggestion as seriously as if he believed in it himself. "So now—absent-mindedly again, you might say," he concluded, "you'll just return it to us. You understand?"

"They don't understand because they never saw your envelope!" Bert answered.

"I could help them to understand, boss," Dan offered quickly. "It would be a pleasure!"

"They're asking for it," his boss said.

"I don't like to hear that kind of suggestion," the

smooth voice said instantly. "I'm convinced that persuasion is always more effective than force. Perhaps you weren't persuasive enough, Frank. Perhaps they think a couple of hundred dollars wouldn't be fair repayment for their trouble. I think myself we could do better than that. Say five hundred?"

"You can say a thousand!" Ken told him. "It won't make any difference. We're telling you we never even saw the envelope!"

"And we'll go on telling you—because it's the truth!" Sandy added.

"Haven't you got sense enough to recognize the truth when you hear it?" Bert demanded.

There was a swish of air past Ken's head and a dull crack. Beside him he could hear Bert's gasp.

"Now maybe you'll shut up, big mouth," Dan said, "until you can say something useful. Any more of your—"

His boss's hoarse voice cut him off. "I'll tell you when we want your help, Dan," the man said gruffly. "Right now I want you and Vic to get them down into the cellar."

An instant later Ken felt himself being tugged to his feet and shoved forward. Then he was halted abruptly and turned to the right. He guessed he was facing the open door of the truck.

"Jump!" Vic ordered him. The palm of a hand thrust roughly against Ken's shoulder.

Ken knew the drop could not be more than a few

feet. But with his eyes blindfolded he had little sense of balance. The rough ground seemed to meet his feet with unexpected force, and he toppled forward. Again a hand grabbed him, pulled him erect, and jerked him sideways.

Another pair of feet landed heavily on the ground beside Ken, and then there was a third thud that told him Sandy and Bert were both out of the truck.

"All right," the hoarse voice said. "Each of you take one of them."

A hand fastened on Ken's arm above the elbow, and propelled him forward. The height of the shoulder that jostled his own told him that either Chet or Dan was serving as his personal guard.

"That's my own little form of persuasion poking you in the back," a voice said close to his ear.

Ken recognized the voice as Dan's, and knew that a gun barrel had been pressed against his back. Helplessly, he stumbled forward over treacherously uneven ground. A heavy growth of high grass or weeds caught at his ankles. The viselike grip on his arm never loosened.

"Stop here," Dan said finally.

Somewhere close in front of him Ken heard the creaking of a door, and immediately afterward a whiff of dank cellar air swept upward across his face.

The hand on Ken's arm thrust him forward again. "Two steps more," Dan said. "And then down."

One step. Two steps. Then Ken's extended foot

was over nothingness, and he stretched it cautiously downward.

"Go on," Dan urged impatiently. "Four more."

The steps were stone. At the bottom of them Ken knew he was standing on a cement floor. He was tugged forward across it for a dozen steps, and then he waited again while another door creaked open.

The musty air beyond the second door made Ken think instantly of rats and spiders.

"Stand there. Don't move!" Dan's hand left Ken's arm as he spoke.

Ken obeyed. He sensed that the room he was in was small, and that to rush forward, or to the right or left, would probably bring him up against a stone wall. To turn and try to make his way out would be equally futile. At his back he could hear the shuffling footsteps that told him Bert and Sandy were also being led into this underground chamber.

Then brisker footsteps sounded, and the man who had called himself Earnest spoke in his usual smooth voice. "This is your last chance," he said almost regretfully. "But before we ask you for the final time where that envelope is, I want to tell you exactly how we know that you must have it in your possession.

"We know," he continued, "that it was put into your car yesterday—under the floor mat in front, on the right side. From that moment on someone was following you. Your car remained constantly in his

sight until you drove it into the parking area behind
the newspaper office in Brentwood late yesterday
afternoon. You were followed again when, shortly
afterward, you took the car to a service station. We
were in that station last night, searching your car,
and the envelope had already been removed. The
conclusion is perfectly obvious, you see. You took the
envelope out of the car when you entered the newspaper office. You put it somewhere for safekeeping,
perhaps waiting for us to make you an offer for it."

He paused briefly. "Well," he said, "we have made
that offer. And I warn you we will not raise it. But I
think under the circumstances you may now be willing to accept our terms. Am I right?"

"But we don't have it!" Ken's voice, raised in
desperation, bounced hollowly back at him from
stone walls.

"All right. You've had your way." The boss's hoarse
voice was directed at the man who had just addressed
the boys. Then it came nearer and spoke so close to
Ken's face that he could feel the man's breath on his
cheek. "Now we'll try another brand of persuasion.
And I think maybe mine will work!"

"Frank! Wait!" the other man said. "Give them ten
minutes to think over what I've said. I'm sure they're
intelligent. They'll see reason if you just give them a
little time."

The boss hesitated. "All right," he said then abruptly. "But ten minutes is all they'll have. Maybe it

won't even seem that long to them. If they get to thinking about what may happen to them if they don't remember—"

"How can they remember?" Bert shouted. "How many times do we have to tell you they don't—"

The dull sound of a landing fist cut off Bert's voice. A second later Ken heard the thud of Bert's body falling heavily to the floor.

"That'll keep him quiet, boss," Dan said with satisfaction. "And maybe it'll kind of help the others to remember a little quicker too."

"We'll leave them alone now," the boss's hoarse voice announced. "We'll be back in—" He paused, and Ken wondered if he was actually cold-blooded enough to be looking at his watch. "Yes," the man rasped, "we'll be back in exactly nine minutes."

Then a heavy door slammed shut, and Ken knew that he and Sandy and Bert were alone.

CHAPTER VI

KEN BLUNDERS

"BERT!" Ken said softly, as the sound of the closing door echoed into silence.

"Bert? Can you hear me?" Sandy's voice spoke at the same time. "Are you all right?"

There was no answer.

"What's happened to him?" Sandy choked on the words. "And where is he? I can't—!"

Ken had lowered himself to his knees, and bent first forward and then to the left and to the right. Now, as a faint sound caught his ear, he moved farther to the right. "I'm beside him, Sandy," he said quickly. "I can hear his breathing. It's steady! He's all right! He'll come to in a minute."

Slowly he straightened, reached backward with his bound hands until they touched a stone wall, and moved rearward until he could lean against it. "Sandy," he said then, "think! We've got to have an answer for them when they come back. We've got to! If we can tell them where that envelope is, they'll let us go. Then we can get Bert out of here. Otherwise—"

He swallowed the further words he had almost spoken. Sandy would know, as well as he knew himself, that all three of them would be at the mercy of their captors if they could not solve an apparently insoluble problem in nine brief minutes.

Their captors were ruthless. The brutal blow that had felled Bert, the words of the man with the hoarse voice, had told them that.

"Think, Sandy!" Ken repeated desperately.

Then, hearing the rising panic in his voice, Ken clenched his teeth and fought for control.

"But what's the good of thinking?" Sandy demanded. His own voice was shrill and thin too. "We never saw their envelope! How can we possibly figure out where it is? Why don't they just believe us when we tell them we don't know? They must be crazy! That's it, Ken! They must be crazy! And they've got us shut up down here—!"

"Sandy! Stop!" The terror in Sandy's voice had somehow helped Ken to regain mastery of himself. As if standing erect might help him face their predicament with more courage, he flung his head up and back. An instant later he gasped in agony. The back of his skull had cracked against a sharp projection of the stone forming the cellar wall. Waves of pain swept over him, and he felt sick and faint.

"Ken!" Sandy said sharply. He had heard the gasp.

"What happened to you?" Concern for his friend had replaced some of his own wild panic.

"I—hit my head—on the stone," Ken managed. "I'm—all right," he added, taking a deep breath. "Never mind me. They're not crazy, you know," he went on carefully. "They really think we've hidden that envelope. So it must have been in our car and—somehow—it was removed. We've got to think how. We've got to figure out where it can be!"

"Yes," Sandy said. "I know." He caught his breath and let it out in a long shuddering sigh. "I've stopped panicking," he added quietly. "I'm trying to think, Ken. But I don't even know where to begin! And we haven't got much time!"

Ken tried to pretend he hadn't heard Sandy's last words. Somewhere inside his own head, at the heart of the throbbing pain there, a clock seemed to be ticking away, measuring off the seconds one by one. He didn't want to listen to it. He began to talk to cover up the sound, without any idea of what he was going to say.

"We'll begin," he said, "at—at—" And suddenly his mind cleared a little. "We'll begin at that restaurant on the turnpike yesterday," he said steadily. "We know the envelope was still in the car there, because they said we'd been followed ever since the thing was planted on us, and that's where they made their first attempt to get it out."

"All right," Sandy said. He continued from where

Ken had left off. "After we left the restaurant we drove straight to the office. The only time the car stopped was when we paid the toll as we left the highway, and at the two red lights in Brentwood."

"We can forget those stops," Ken said. "Nobody could have got anything out of the car then. And we didn't even open the doors, so nothing could have fallen out." The pain in his head had gradually localized to one pounding, throbbing spot right beneath the hard knot in the towel tied around his head. If he could only shift that knot, he thought—

"Right," Sandy was saying. "And at the office we parked alongside the open door to the pressroom. So it's almost certain nobody could have tampered with the car then."

If he could only shift that knot! Ken thought. He could feel a trickle of sweat begin to run down his brow. Aloud he said, through clenched teeth, "So the envelope must have been in the car when we took it to Joe's service station for repairs."

That rock projection on which he had cracked his head! Ken thought suddenly. If he could catch the knot on that point he might be able to shift it a little. Cautiously he leaned back against the wall, touched it with his head, and moved a careful inch to the right. Then another inch.

"That must be where it disappeared," Sandy was saying. "It's got to be! Or they'd have found it when they broke into the gas station last night to search the car. Joe and his big robbery," he added with a groan. "We sit there listening to him tell us all about it and we don't have the sense to guess—"

Ken missed Sandy's next few words. He had located the small pointed projection, had tilted his head so that the knot was just above it, and then pulled his head down slightly. The knot moved! The pain was excruciating, but Ken persisted.

And then suddenly the pained eased. He had moved the knot far enough to give him some relief.

He took a deep breath.

"—and if Tony Canzoni had picked them up then, we wouldn't be here now," Sandy was saying.

"There's no use going all over that," Ken said.

"There's no use going over anything!" Sandy answered. "How can we possibly guess who was wandering around Joe's station before it closed last night, poking into our car?"

"But Joe was working on the car himself," Ken pointed out. "So he'd certainly notice anybody who even came close to it."

"Sure! But just tell that to those stupid crooks!"

"Cut it out, Sandy!" Ken said sharply. The startling thought had just crossed his mind that at least one of their captors might have been left in the room with them—that he was standing now only a few feet away, intent on learning anything that Ken and Sandy meant to conceal from the men who held them prisoner. And calling those men names, Ken knew, might make their own situation even more serious. "The envelope!" He prodded. "Just keep thinking about the envelope! Isn't there any way it could have been taken out of the car before we drove over to Joe's to—"

"Ken!" The single word was almost a shout.

"What is it? Sandy—are you all right?"

"Sure—sure! It's just that I think I know what may have happened to it!" Sandy was talking so fast Ken could barely follow him. "Listen now! When we took the car in—"

A faint groan sounded near their feet.

Sandy broke off abruptly. "Bert?" he cried. "Bert? Can you hear me?"

"It's us, Bert—Sandy and Ken," Ken said quickly. If Bert was returning to consciousness he would have no idea where he was. He would know only that he was apparently blind, and that his hands were tied behind his back.

"Where—? What—?" Bert's voice sounded weak and confused.

"We're still down in that cellar, Bert," Ken told him. "But Sandy thinks he may have an idea—"

"Oh! The cellar. Now I remember." With every word Bert's voice grew stronger. "The next time I meet that loudmouthed thug with my hands untied I'll—"

"Bert, wait a minute," Ken broke in. "We haven't much time. They said they'd let us out of here if we could tell them where that envelope is. And Sandy just said he thought he had it figured out. Go ahead, Sandy—tell us what you were going to say."

"Bert—are you all right? Is there anything—" Sandy broke off.

"Go ahead," his brother ordered. "I'm even trying to sit up now. Forget about me. If you've thought of something that will get us out of here—talk!"

"I was thinking of the work Joe did on our car, Ken," Sandy began, and once more he was rattling his words off at top speed. "And I realized he checked the fluid in the automatic transmission. Didn't he?"

"Yes, sure. But—" Ken's puzzlement suddenly gave way to illumination. As if someone had pulled up a window shade, he saw clearly what Sandy was driving at. "You've got it!"

"Talk sense, you two!" Bert begged. "What's your automatic transmission got to do with . . . ?"

"It is sense, Bert!" Ken broke in. "To get at our oil-filler plug Joe had to lift the floor mat in the front of the car—the floor mat on the right side! Get it?"

"Don't you see, Bert?" Sandy said. "That's exactly where—"

"I get it!" The strength of hope surged through Bert's voice as he said the words. "That's where they said they hid their envelope!"

"So Joe must have seen it and taken it out!" Sandy

hurried on. "And we know he didn't put it back when he quit work last night—or the men would have found it when they searched the car."

"But wait a minute!" Bert sounded suddenly doubtful. "Joe's a careful guy. If he'd found something in your car, he'd have laid it aside to give to you—if he didn't put it right back where he found it, that is. So if he found it, why didn't he turn it over to you when you picked up the car?"

"Probably because he was all steamed up about somebody having broken into the garage," Ken said quickly. "He rushed over to tell us about his robbery the minute we arrived. And then we got to teasing him about his big story—and by the time we left— Anyway," he concluded, "the envelope is probably lying on Joe's workbench right now!"

"Or he's noticed it there by now," Sandy added, "and put it away somewhere to keep for us. Let's start yelling," he added. "Let's get those guys in here right now and tell them where their envelope is! I want to get out of this place!"

"Hang on, Sandy," Bert said. "We'd better go over this thing once more and make sure of what we're going to say. Something tells me we're not going to get out of here anyway until those guys actually have that envelope in their hands. And if we send them off on a wild-goose chase—we'll just be cooking our own goose," Bert added with grim humor. "Come on. Take it once more from the beginning."

"But—! Well, all right." Reluctantly Sandy accepted Bert's reasoning, and began again to rattle off the facts and deductions which had brought him to his conclusion: that the mysterious envelope was at that moment on Joe's workbench or on the desk in the garage owner's little office.

Ken was listening to him, head bent, his whole mind focused on what Sandy was saying. Suddenly he became aware of a streak of white in the total darkness to which he had become accustomed during the last agonizing moments. For a split second he didn't understand its significance. Then he realized that he was seeing a strip of his own shirt front. And he knew that when he had pushed at his blindfold, to ease the pain in his head, he had gained for himself the ability to see a little of what was directly below his eyes.

Until that moment he had assumed that the cellar had been left dark when the men departed. Now he knew there must be at least a faint light in it. Automatically he tilted his head back, to discover what else he could see.

As he did so he realized that he might be able to outwit the determination of their jailer to conceal his identity. If he could get one good look at the man the others referred to as "the boss"—the man who had gone to so much trouble to preserve his anonymity—he might recognize the face. Ken had trained himself to remember faces he had seen, even those he had seen only in photographs. And if the "boss" was, as Ken suspected, a well-known criminal, it was likely that the man's picture had appeared either in a newspaper or a police rogues gallery.

But no! It was no use.

With his head tilted back Ken discovered that he could see nothing at all but a tiny patch of light on either side of his nose.

If only he had pushed the blindfold farther out of place he might—

He decided to ask Sandy to use his bound hands to move the blindfold another fraction of an inch. Sandy could reach it if Ken crouched down behind him.

In almost the same breath Ken changed his mind. He knew he did not dare risk seeking Sandy's help. Their allotted number of minutes, he thought, must be almost gone. At any second the men would re-enter the room. And if, when they came in, Sandy was trying to dislodge Ken's blindfold—

No, it would be too dangerous.

Perhaps, Ken thought, he could move the blindfold again himself.

He was no longer hearing Sandy's recital, and Bert's occasional comments. He was too busy.

First he found once more the small projection of rock that had been useful to him earlier. Then he maneuvered his head until the tightly bound cloth was just above it. Then, as he had done before, he pulled his head slightly downward. The blindfold shifted, but only infinitesimally.

Ken turned his head a little and repeated the performance. Again the blindfold moved slightly. Now it no longer lay evenly across his eyes. Now it had slipped upward on his left temple. Now the strip of light he could see was a little larger.

Twice more he let the point of rock shift the cloth.

That time, when he looked down, he could actually see the tip of his own shoes on the dirt floor.

He caught his breath in triumph.

Moving his head sideways he brought Sandy's moccasins into view.

He opened his mouth to let the others know what he had accomplished, but Bert's voice forestalled him.

"What do you think, Ken?" Bert asked. "Sandy's convinced me that the envelope must be either on Joe's bench or in his office. Shall we yell and try to bring the men in here and tell them that? The sooner we—"

The sound of a door creaking open cut Bert off short.

"No need to call us." The words were spoken by the rough voice of the man the others called boss.

Footsteps thudded on the cement floor. The men were re-entering the room.

"We heard everything you said," the man went on.

"The partition of this room doesn't go up to the ceiling."

"Yeah, we heard everything!" Ken recognized the voice of Dan. "So I'm a loudmouthed thug, am I?"

Ken could visualize the man glowering down at Bert.

The man with the smooth voice spoke up quickly. "This is no time to take offense at a little understandable name-calling, Dan," he said. "Your behavior toward this young man wasn't what could be called courteous. Yes," he went on, and Ken realized that the man was now speaking to Bert and Sandy and himself, "we overheard everything. And we want to congratulate all three of you on the thoroughness with which you thought through your problem."

"You can be glad we listened to you," the boss said gruffly.

"That's right," the smooth voice added. "We can trust you now, you see—just as I felt certain all along that we could. And as soon as we have recovered our envelope, you will be free to leave with our thanks— and with that payment we promised you."

While Ken listened with one part of his mind, he held his head tilted backward and at an angle. Already he had been able to see three pairs of shoes. But the direction of the voices that had spoken suggested that none of them belonged to the man the others called their boss. That was the man whose face he was determined to see. One quick look might tell him all he wanted to know.

"You understand we can't guarantee that the envelope is still in the service station," Bert was saying evenly. "All we can say is that that's where we think it must be."

"It had better be there!" Dan growled.

"But if the owner of the service station has taken it home—" Sandy began.

"If it's not there," Bert interrupted him quickly, and Ken knew he hoped to keep Joe Meyers safely out of the situation, "we don't know where it is. And there won't be any use asking us about it any longer. You already know everything we can tell you."

"If it's not at the service station," the boss rasped, "we'll send one of you out to find it. And we'll keep the other two right here as hostages, you might say— to make sure the one we choose to do the errand doesn't get any bright ideas, like calling the police. But we'll try the service station first—and you'd better hope we find it there."

While the man talked, Ken faced in the direction of the voice. The moment he did so he saw a fourth pair of shoes—black ones, with a high polish.

"That's the one!" he thought triumphantly. "That's the boss who is so afraid he might be seen—or that someone might mention his name!"

Slowly he tipped his head farther back, to raise the narrow strip of his vision.

He saw the man's knees, and a big heavy hand with a diamond winking on one finger.

"Oh, sure, we'll try the service station, boss," Dan was saying. "But if the thing isn't there—well, all I can say—"

"You've already said enough, I should think," the smooth voice announced. "I suggest we waste no more time."

Ken could see as high as the man's waist now. He took a deep breath. He was going to have to tip his head still farther back.

"How about removing these blindfolds?" Sandy suggested.

"Oh, come now!" There was a smile in the smooth voice. "We haven't really subjected you to any discomfort. Surely you can bear your situation for a little longer—when you think of how handsomely you're going to be paid for it."

The boss gave a short unpleasant laugh. "The blinders stay on," he said abruptly. "You can consider yourself lucky that I haven't let Dan and Chet here give you a little taste of their favorite exercise."

"Now—now!" the smooth voice objected. "We weren't going to have any talk like that."

Ken could see the man's chest now. Only a little bit farther, he told himself, and he would see the face.

Just then a hand flashed across his field of vision—

a hand holding an open knife that was jabbing directly toward his chest.

Instinctively Ken shrank back, pressing hard against the wall.

"Wise guy!" Dan yelled triumphantly. "I knew it, boss! This wise guy's got his blindfold half pulled off!"

As the words bellowed in Ken's ear, fingers grabbed his shoulder and shook him violently.

Ken pulled sideways, away from the grasp, and ducked. His head brushed roughly against the wall. The loosened blindfold was jerked higher, completely exposing his right eye.

He found himself staring past Dan's shoulder into a heavily lined face that was completely familiar—so familiar that for an instant Ken thought it must belong to someone he saw every day.

Then realization burst upon him. The face was familiar because it so often appeared in newspapers and on television screens. It was the face of a man who had successfully defied law-enforcement agencies for twenty years or more, who had been tried on a dozen serious charges but had always managed to wriggle out of a conviction.

"Frank Thorne!" Ken spoke the name aloud without meaning to.

"Thorne!" The amazed echo came from Bert.

"So! We have an amateur snooper here, eh?" The rough voice was strangely quiet now, and slow, and

Thorne's eyes bored into Ken's. "This changes the situation," the man said. "Yes"—he nodded—"this certainly changes the situation!"

Ken knew then what he had done.

A moment earlier Bert and Sandy and he had almost certainly faced nothing more than another hour of discomfort—and the knowledge that they had been tricked and used by a criminal gang.

Now the menace in the deep-set eyes and the quiet words of Frank Thorne told Ken that he had placed himself and his friends in deadly peril.

Strange things happened to people who possessed information that could be dangerous to Frank Thorne.

CHAPTER VII

RACE AGAINST MINUTES

IT was the smooth-spoken man who broke the stifling silence. "That was most unfortunate, young man—most unfortunate," he said.

His face was indistinguishable to Ken in the dim light of a small bulb on the ceiling, but his manner was only quietly regretful, as if he were reproving Ken for some slight and trivial fault.

"Because," the man added, "as Thorne says, it does change things."

Dan moved his knife a fraction of an inch closer to Ken's chest. "But we can take care of the situation, can't we, boss?" The man said over his shoulder.

"Get away from him, Dan," Thorne said curtly.

Dan looked surprised. Reluctantly he took a step backward.

"Yes, Dan," the smooth voice said. "This is no time for your crude methods. This—"

"This is no time for talk, Randall," Thorne cut in. "And no place for it, either."

Randall? Randall? The name repeated itself in Ken's brain. He could remember no man named Randall who had ever been known to associate with Thorne.

"We've wasted enough time," Thorne was saying. "Right now we're going to go and get that envelope," he announced flatly. At last he took his eyes from Ken's face to look first at the man he had called Randall and then at the three underlings to whom he was always "the boss."

"I want no slip-ups tonight," Thorne went on. "This time I don't want any cops nosing around that place before we've had a chance to find what we're looking for. If it's there," he added, and once more his eyes stabbed briefly into Ken's. "So this time we'll all go. I'll tell each of you what he's got to do while we're on the way."

"But we're not goin' to leave them here alone, are we, boss?" Chet asked, jerking his thumb toward Bert, who was still seated on the floor, and then toward Sandy and Ken.

"They'll be all right," Thorne said. "Just tape their ankles up good and tight, in case they were thinking of taking a stroll before we get back. And stick some tape on their mouths too," he added. "But be careful about it!" he warned sharply. "I don't want them marked up."

"Randall!" The name burst out of Bert suddenly. "You're the Randall who was mixed up in that stock

deal a year ago! The federal authorities looked into
the case and—"

Randall laughed. "More amateur snooping, I see."
Then he raised his head arrogantly, so that the dim
light illuminated a thin hawklike nose and thin lips
in a narrow face. "That was mere talk," he said
brusquely. "Nothing was ever proved against me."

"But this is no stock deal you're mixed up in now,"
Bert said, turning his blindfolded eyes straight toward the man who had associated himself with
Frank Thorne. "Right now you're risking more than
an investigation if you—"

A piece of adhesive tape stuck roughly across
Bert's mouth cut short his words.

"You talk too much," Dan said, stepping back
briefly to admire his handiwork before he began to
tape Bert's ankles.

At a gesture from Thorne his other two henchmen
went to work on Ken and Sandy too.

Ken was shoved roughly down on the floor, and
then Chet began to lash tape around his ankles. Ken
could see Bert and Sandy, to his right, their blindfolds still in place, being subjected to a similar truss-
ing. Within a few minutes all three of them were
securely bound and gagged.

"Almost forgot this!" Chet said with a laugh, pulling off Ken's dislodged blindfold and untying it.
"Wouldn't want you to feel neglected, sonny," he

"Don't go away," Dan said jeeringly

added, placing the cloth once more across Ken's eyes. "No, sir! We want to treat you all alike."

"Hurry up!" Thorne snapped.

"Just about done, boss," Chet assured him, knotting the cloth.

"Come along then," Thorne commanded, "and turn off the light."

Ken knew that Dan was the last to leave the room, because it was Dan's voice that said jeeringly, "Don't go away," just before a door slammed shut.

The mocking words seemed to repeat themselves over and over in Ken's head. "Don't go away!"

Ken felt himself begin to tremble. Every precaution had been taken to ensure that Bert and Sandy and he would still be lying helpless on the cellar floor when Thorne and Randall and the other three men returned. And Ken knew with a terrible clarity what would take place then. Now that Thorne had been recognized, the man's safety depended on the silence of his three captives. And men like Thorne knew just one way to ensure silence.

Somewhere outside a car engine roared into life. An instant later the engine was muted, and gradually the sound of it died away. Thorne and the others were on their way to Joe Meyers' garage.

They had not injured Bert and Sandy and Ken before they left. If they didn't find the envelope in the garage they would question their prisoners further when they returned.

But if they did find the envelope . . .

The choking silence in the underground room was broken by a scraping, rustling noise. It came from Ken's right. He knew immediately that either Bert or Sandy was twisting and struggling, exerting all his strength in an effort to rip the tape that bound his wrists together.

"Mmm! Mmm!" The grunted protest, from behind taped lips, came from close beside Ken.

That meant, Ken knew, that it was Bert who was trying to force his bonds. It was Sandy who was endeavoring, wordlessly, to urge his brother to give up the useless struggle.

Swiftly Ken added his own grunted appeal. "Mmm! Mmm!" With all his will he tried to force meaning into the senseless sounds. Bert couldn't shear those layers of adhesive, no matter how hard he tried. He must be warned to save his strength for some effort more hopeful of success. "Mmm! Mmm!"

A single exhausted gasp was Ken's answer. Bert was pitting his muscles against the taped bonds no longer. Now only his labored breathing could be heard over Sandy's lighter quicker breath and the pounding of Ken's own blood in his ears.

If they had time enough, Ken thought desperately, they might devise some method of releasing each other.

But how much time would they have?

How long had it taken them, he wondered, to be

brought to this place in the closed truck? How far was their cellar prison from the diner on the highway, where they had been captured?

Had the trip taken twenty minutes? Twenty-five minutes? Half an hour?

It was impossible to guess. Every moment of the journey had been filled with tension. It might have lasted ten minutes. It might have lasted an hour. Ken realized he could never make a trustworthy estimate.

And it was impossible to guess how long Thorne and his men would spend in Joe's garage. If they broke in without difficulty—and Ken thought grimly that Dan and Chet and Vic were all undoubtedly skilled at that sort of task—and found the envelope on Joe's workbench or in his office, they might be driving away from the garage within three minutes after they reached it.

Ken shook his head furiously. He was wasting precious moments. Whether they had less than thirty minutes, or more than sixty, they should be spending every second of it in an active effort to free themselves.

If they succeeded before their captors returned, they might yet live to see Frank Thorne pay for all his past and present misdeeds.

If they were discovered, on their captors' return, still struggling to break their bonds, they could scarcely face a worse fate than the one Ken felt certain was already in store for them.

But how could they free themselves?

Ken forced himself to concentrate his thoughts on the contents of his pockets. Did he possess anything that could be used to cut or tear through strong adhesive tape?

In the inside top pocket of his jacket, he knew, were a small comb and two pencils.

In the outer top jacket pocket was a handkerchief.

In the lower right jacket pocket were a key ring and few odd coins.

There was more loose change in the side pocket of his slacks. And in the hip pocket was his wallet.

Silently he listed each item, and silently discarded each one as useless.

Only the keys offered a glimmer of hope, but he knew it would take hours to saw through adhesive tape with the dull edge of a key.

If neither Sandy nor Bert had anything more useful, then they would have to make an attempt with the keys. But first—

Ken heaved his cramped body toward the right. By using his knees and the finger tips of his bound hands, he managed to push himself into a sideways roll. Once more he made the same violent effort. And that time, as he completed the roll, he felt himself come up against the solid bulk of Sandy's body.

Swiftly Ken twisted again, until his back was toward Sandy and his bound hands could touch Sandy's side.

For a split second Sandy held himself rigid. Then he shifted with a convulsive movement. An instant later Ken felt Sandy's fingers touching his own.

Now they lay on the cellar floor back to back, bound hands touching.

Immediately one of Sandy's fingers began a slow, uneven series of taps against Ken's hand—taps that Ken recognized as the dots and dashes of the Morse code.

Ken caught his breath in relief, to know that Sandy and he were in contact, each—Ken was sure—concentrating on a single goal. Then Ken cleared his mind of everything but the sensation in his hands—the taps communicated to him by Sandy's fingers.

"H-a-v-e—y-o-u—k-n-i-f-e?" Sandy tapped out.

Ken's heart sank.

The question told him, as clearly as if Sandy had spoken it aloud, that Sandy himself had no knife or any other object capable of cutting through tough tape.

Swiftly Ken tapped back the signal for No, and then he added, "D-o-e-s—B-e-r-t?"

Ken interpreted a jerk of Sandy's body as a shrug indicating Sandy's ignorance.

For a moment their two pairs of hands touched, motionless. Ken knew Sandy must be remembering, as he himself was doing, that Bert did not know the Morse code. This meant that Sandy could not signal his brother a question on the subject.

"S-e-a-r-c-h—h-i-m," Ken suggested.

Sandy wasted no time signaling a response. Instead, he rolled away from Ken, edging his body toward Bert's.

How many minutes Ken lay alone after that in the dark, out of contact with the Allens, he didn't know. The rustle of cloth against cloth told him that Sandy was prompting his brother to turn this way and that, so that his pockets might be explored.

Finally Sandy's body rolled back against Ken's and his fingers tapped out a single short dismaying word.

"N-o."

Feverishly Ken drove his thoughts back to other occasions when Sandy and he had escaped from imprisoning bonds. How had they managed then? he asked himself. What had they used? Had they had knives to aid them then, or—?

Glass! The word thundered inside his head.

That was the answer. A sliver of glass could cut almost as well as a knife.

But what did they have with them now that was made of glass?

A wrist-watch crystal?

Ken discarded the thought as soon as it occurred to him. The crystal on his own watch was made of an unbreakable plastic. Sandy's and Bert's were identical.

And none of them wore glasses.

But Sandy often used sunglasses when he was driving! Ken remembered with a sudden surge of hope. And so did Bert.

If, by some lucky chance, one of them had those glasses in a pocket now. . . .

Ken's fingers began to tap out a frantic message. With Sandy he never had to waste words in explanation. The message said only, "B-r-e-a-k—s-u-n-g-l-a-s-s-e-s."

For a split second Sandy didn't respond, and Ken knew he was mentally checking his own pockets again. Then Sandy's fingers signaled, "N-e-e-d—B-e-r-t'-s."

Once more Sandy rolled away from Ken, toward the figure of his brother.

This time Ken tried to curb his wild impatience by counting off seconds.

It didn't help. Each second that passed was a terrifying reminder of how little time might remain in which to manage their escape. And so far they had accomplished nothing. Nothing!

How many more seconds would they have, Ken wondered, before the sound of an approaching car signaled the return of Thorne and the others?

Asking himself that question was no help, either.

Was Bert doing his best to help Sandy? Ken asked of the darkness. Or had Bert failed to understand what Sandy was after, and was he instead unwittingly adding to the difficulties of Sandy's search?

Uselessly Ken wished that either he or Sandy possessed the desperately needed pair of glasses. They had been in trouble together more than once in the past, and their shared experiences had given them an instinctive ability to co-operate—an ability that sometimes functioned almost automatically and without the need for communication. If Sandy had a pair of sunglasses at this moment, he would know how to move to put them within the most convenient reach of Ken's groping fingers. If necessary, he could even tell Ken how best to reach them, by tapping out a terse message.

Ken felt sweat chill on his forehead as his fear and impatience mounted. Behind the choking gag he labored for breath.

And then, at last, Sandy rolled against him.

As if a skillful hand had administered oxygen, Ken was himself again, tense but alert for his friend's signal.

He felt something smooth slide between his hands. He knew his fingers were closing on a pair of glasses.

There was no need for further tapped signals. Ken knew Sandy would not have given him the glasses unless he expected him to be the one to make use of them. Sandy's gesture said silently, "You take the glasses. You use them on me."

Breathing a silent thanks for the good fortune that had put the potential tool in Bert's pocket, Ken held the glasses between rigid fingers for a moment, to make certain that his grip on them was secure.

Then he rolled over on his back, so that his bound hands, with the glasses between them, were pinned beneath him. He took a single deep breath, and arched his back.

He separated his fingers, letting the glasses fall to the floor, and pulled his hands up away from them, toward the small of his back.

Then he let his body drop hard, driving the base of his spine against the spot where he hoped the glasses lay. A painful jab told him that the weight of his body had come down on the right spot.

But had he broken the glass into splinters big enough to pick up and use?

Fearfully Ken arched his back once more and moved his hands along the hard dirt floor.

Suddenly his hands jerked involuntarily, pulling back from the splinter that had sent a stab of agony through the base of his right thumb. But a moment later his fumbling fingers, returning to their task, had fastened on a sizable glass sliver.

Sternly he quelled the temptation to turn toward Sandy. One splinter would probably not be enough to finish the difficult task that lay ahead. It might break, or fall and elude his search. And once he had moved away from the broken pair of glasses, he might not be able to find them again without long moments of seeking.

Carefully he groped over the ground for the space

of several more seconds, until he held three usable splinters in his hands.

Then, finally, he rolled over onto his side, and thrust his hands backward toward Sandy's.

"H-o-l-d—e-x-t-r-a—p-i-e-c-e-s," he tapped out.

Obediently Sandy spread his fingers and Ken managed to slide two of the tiny glass blades between them. Sandy carefully closed his hands on the precious objects.

Ken took a new firm grip on the single sliver of glass he still held. Carefully he felt for the edge of the wrapping around Sandy's wrists. Carefully he drew the sharp glass point from that edge across the width of the bound layers of tape.

The glass made a faint scraping sound in the silence.

Ken shifted the glass to the upper edge of the binding and drew it across the tape again. And then again. And then again.

Ken knew that he sometimes missed, and jabbed into Sandy's flesh. The quivers of Sandy's body told him that. But the redhead always steadied his hands instantly after each convulsive jerk, and Ken forced himself to keep going.

The edges of the little glass sliver cut into Ken's skin too. When the glass became harder and harder to hold, in fingers that seemed to grow more slippery with each moment, he didn't know if his hands were wet with sweat or with blood.

Time crawled. Time raced. Again and again and again Ken drew the tiny sliver across the tape.

When he had counted off a hundred strokes he paused for an instant, to ease cramped muscles. Hopefully he felt the surface of the tape to judge what progress he had made.

All he could detect was a faint roughness. Not a single layer of the tape had yet been cut through.

Grimly Ken returned to the seemingly hopeless task.

Now he tried to move more quickly. But his fingers tired so rapidly that he had to stop to rest before he had made another hundred strokes.

He clenched his teeth, tried to wipe off the slippery bit of glass on the sleeve of Sandy's coat, and started once more.

Suddenly the glass was gone. He hadn't been conscious of dropping it. He just knew that it was no longer in his fingers.

He took a long shivering breath, tapped the back of Sandy's hand, and accepted the new sliver that Sandy passed to him.

He had long ago stopped counting his strokes. Now he had no idea of how many times he had dragged the bit of glass across the tape. His motions had become mechanical. He felt as if his hands had been moving back and forth in that same gesture forever.

At last he stopped and felt the tape once more.

A strangled cry of victory caught in his throat. The tape had been cut through at the upper edge. And at least half the surface of the top layer had apparently been deeply frayed.

The meager success gave him new strength. Holding the glass in his left hand, he jammed the first two fingers of his right hand beneath the cut edge of the tape, took a deep breath, and pulled as hard as he could.

Even over the pounding of his own pulse he could hear the split-second sound of the tape ripping for a brief fraction of an inch. Then it held fast again.

Trying to transfer the glass shard from his left hand back to his right, he dropped it.

For a moment he lay still, not sure he could tackle the exhausting task again. Then he tapped Sandy's fingers, received the third sliver, and set to work once more. He was aware that he was using the last piece of glass. If he dropped this one—

Back and forth he sawed now, across the lower barely scarred section of tape. Back and forth. Back and forth. Again he lost track of time. Again he had become an automaton mechanically performing a task that had lost all meaning.

Sandy's suddenly tapping fingers finally halted him in mid-stroke.

Ken managed to collect his wits just in time to interpret Sandy's message. The tapping fingers signaled, "W-a-i-t."

The one word was enough. Ken knew what Sandy was going to do. The redhead was going to attempt to rip through the remainder of the uncut tape by sheer strength.

Ken didn't try to argue with him. It was just possible that Sandy could manage it.

Ken knew the agony his friend would endure, when he twisted his lacerated wrists against the adhesive. But he knew too that Sandy, like himself, realized that their time might be growing short.

Ken rolled slightly away from his friend, to give him more room. Then, still holding tightly to the last sharp blade of glass, he waited.

Sandy sucked in a deep breath. Ken could visualize him, as he let that breath out in short gasps, scissoring one wrist against the other, trying to use the advantage of the ripped edge to carry the tear across the full width of the wrapping.

Ken gritted his teeth, as if he himself were sharing the pain.

Then he heard it—the sound of ripping. It stopped almost as soon as it started. But an instant later it started again.

And suddenly Sandy, who had been lying on his side, fell heavily over onto his back. The breath whooshing out of his body, in a final gasp, was a sound of triumph.

Then Ken felt a single heavy limp hand fall on his own arm.

Sandy's hands were freed!

The big redhead lay motionless for only a few seconds, sucking in air through his nostrils.

A rustling sound told Ken that he was sitting up. Again Ken could follow vividly, in his own imagination, the gestures of Sandy's bleeding limp fingers as he clawed at the tape over his mouth.

The tape came off in two agonizing tugs.

"Ah-h-h!" It was a cry of pain. But it was a cry of triumph too.

An instant later Sandy croaked, "Now! Just a second! Ken—your hands!"

Ken had already thrust them out. While Sandy worked over the strips of tape he told his brother, "Be with you in a minute, Bert." He was grunting with the effort. "As soon as I—get your hands free— we'll all go to work on our ankles. We'll get out of here yet!"

Ken was scarcely aware of it when the binding around his wrists finally came free. Sandy had to jolt the nearly paralyzed hands to thrust them apart.

"Come on!" Sandy said. There was almost a grin in his voice. "Get moving!"

Ken rubbed his fingers, trying to restore their circulation, before he even reached for the tape over his mouth. Sandy was already beside Bert.

Pulling off the gag felt like slashing his face with a knife. But Ken ignored the pain and concentrated on forcing his numb fingers to tackle the job of removing the layers of tape that bound his ankles together.

"Whew!" The gasp of relief told Ken that Bert's gag was gone too. "How'd you get your hands free to—?"

"We'll talk later," Sandy interrupted. "Free your ankles."

Side by side in the darkness—Ken had not realized until he pulled off his blindfold that the cellar's one light had been extinguished—they groaned and sweated.

"They certainly used enough of this stuff!" Sandy muttered once. "Maybe we could hop out of here."

"We couldn't get very far, hopping," Ken reminded him, jerking at the rugged tape. "And we may have to run for it—if we're able to move at all before they get back."

"Right," Sandy agreed tersely. "You almost finished?"

"I am—almost," Bert said. "And the first thing we do when we get out of here is to head for a phone. Maybe we can get Andy Kane here in time to round up those hoodlums."

"I'm standing up!" Sandy announced abruptly, some time later. For a moment his feet shuffled against the floor, as he tried to restore their feeling. Then he said, "Let me give a hand, Ken. Your fingers probably aren't much use yet."

Ken could hear Bert get to his feet too, while

Sandy struggled with the last stubborn layer of tape.

"There!" Sandy gasped. "Can you stand up?"

"I'll make it," Ken assured him, getting to his knees first and then coming erect on quivering legs.

"Which way is the door?" Bert wanted to know.

"Right over there," Ken said. "Here—find my hand. Follow me. I saw it before when—"

He broke off. "A car!" he breathed.

For an instant that seemed endless they held their breaths and strained to listen.

They all heard it then—the unmistakable sounds of a car coming up the steep grade to the house.

"We're too late!" Sandy's voice cracked. "We'll never make it now!"

CHAPTER VIII

CORNERED

KEN was moving even as Sandy spoke. Holding both the Allens, each by an arm, he was heading through the darkness toward the place where he felt sure he recalled having seen a door.

Suddenly headlight beams shone through a small dusty window high in the cellar wall. By the yellowish glow they could all see the door, just a few feet away.

Ken reached for it, jerked it open, and managed dimly to see a flight of stairs on the far side of the room they stepped into, before the headlights swung away and left the whole cellar in total darkness once more.

But they had seen their path to the stairs. They took it as swiftly as they dared.

Then they were stumbling up the steps, Ken in the lead, the others close behind. Ken kept one hand stretched out in front of him, and as soon as he touched wood he began to feel around for a door-knob.

For a long terrifying second it eluded him. Then his still awkward fingers closed over a round object. It turned in his hands. The door swung open. Ken stepped over the sill.

Gleaming white surfaces all around him, catching and reflecting the moonlight coming through one window, told him that he was in a kitchen—a sur-prisingly modern kitchen, after the musty cellar they had just left.

A door lock clicked at his back. Sandy and Bert had followed him into the kitchen, and had closed the door at the head of the stairs.

Two dark rectangles in the kitchen wall signaled openings to the outdoors or to other parts of the house.

Ken noticed them just as they all heard a car door slam somewhere toward the front of the house.

"Out the back way!" Ken murmured, and headed for a door which he hoped would lead to safety. Once outside, he was thinking swiftly, they could hide in the shrubbery for a few moments, if necessary, and then make for their car.

Ken pulled open the door on utter darkness. He took one step forward and stubbed his foot. The jolt threw him forward. He found himself half sprawl-ing on a flight of stairs leading upward.

"No good," he whispered over his shoulder, straightening up and backing out into the kitchen again.

"There was another door—over there!" Sandy breathed.

"I know. Come on."

Hands outthrust to guide them around half-seen obstacles, they edged around a table in the center of the room. Ken's foot kicked a low stool which had been invisible half under the table, and he stopped a moment, holding his breath.

"Hurry!" Bert urged. "When they get into the cellar they'll hear every move we make up here!"

Sandy grunted softly as his hip struck the corner of a protruding cupboard which Ken had managed to skirt. From inside it came the rattle of precariously stacked dishes.

Ken was still holding his breath after that close shave when his fingers closed around the knob of the door he had been aiming for.

He turned the knob and pulled on it gently. Nothing happened. The door remained shut.

For a second Ken felt blind panic. Then he pushed the knob. The door moved, creaking.

Ken held it still, barely two inches open.

Carefully he closed both hands around the knob, and this time he pulled upward as he pushed, lifting the door slightly above the threshold against which it had scraped. That time it moved noiselessly and

Ken followed it as it opened. The others were at his back.

Bert, who was in the rear, gently shut the door.

They had entered a big room that seemed to extend the whole width of the house, from front to back. The thin moonlight coming through several large windows showed them its shape, and the shadowy forms of chairs, tables, and other pieces of furniture.

A flashlight bobbed outside a front window.

Instinctively Ken ducked.

But the light did not pierce into the room. Instead, its beam moved around a corner. Ken realized that the man holding the light was walking around the house toward the rear. He saw the flashlight pass one window in the side wall, and then another. Faintly he could hear the voices of the men who had returned from Joe Meyers' garage.

Ken turned his head. The whole rear wall of the room was composed of large French windows extending from floor to ceiling. The area outside them, suddenly illuminated by the flashlight beam, seemed to be a paved garden, or patio—another of the modern touches to this house which had apparently once been a simple farmhouse.

"That's our way out," Ken breathed, close to Sandy's ear. "Through those glass doors. As soon as they start down the cellar—"

He broke off with a gulp, as the flashlight swung

around the corner of the house, angled across the row of transparent doors for a moment, and then turned straight toward the glass.

It seemed impossible that the three occupants of the room had not become suddenly visible to the men outside. Ken, Sandy, and Bert stood frozen, unable to move.

Then the light flicked around again and bobbed on. It was clear that the men beyond the glass doors were unaware that their former prisoners stood only a dozen feet from them, separated from their lights and their guns by only a fragile wall of glass. Like gray shadows, the men moved toward the last of the row of tall windows.

"We'll have about thirty seconds," Sandy was whispering, "before they discover that we're not still in the cellar."

Ken gripped his arm. Sandy fell silent. The flashlight was illuminating the old-fashioned sloping cellar doors at the edge of the patio. But the man holding the light, and the others with him, had suddenly halted. Nobody bent to open the cellar doors. A voice raised in anger became audible through the glass.

"I don't care what you think!" Randall's once smooth tone had roughened. "I'm convinced that every cop in Brentwood was out prowling that road leading out of town."

"Hick-town cops!" Dan said contemptuously.

"Why should you care if they were patrolling the roads? Whatever it is they were looking for, it kept them out of our way!"

"That's right," Chet agreed. "There wasn't a cop within five blocks of that service station. We just walked in and took that envelope off the desk—like taking candy from a baby!"

"All right, boys," Thorne said brusquely. Then he added, "But they're right, Randall. What's worrying you? We don't know what brought the cops out onto the highway—but we don't care!"

"Not even if what they're looking for is that red convertible parked in front of this house?" Randall demanded.

"How could they be looking for that car?" Thorne asked belligerently. "It's only been here for a couple of hours. Nobody would have reported it missing so soon." He struck a match to light a cigar, and in the flare of the light his face looked red and angry. "I've said this before, Randall," he went on. "I'll say it just once more. That car and those three snoopers are my problem. I'll handle it—and without any more help from you. Sure—the cops'll find that car eventually. But when they do it'll be a complete wreck. It's going to run off the road—accidentally, you understand—and wind up wrapped around a tree. And it's passengers aren't going to be doing any talking about how the accident happened."

The light of the match died abruptly, but Thorne's

voice went on. "Your worry, Randall, is the secret Petrane report in that envelope. You said if we could steal that report for you, and give you some capital for a start, you'd make us a million dollars in Petrane stock. Well, you've got the report. The capital's waiting for you when you're ready to use it. Now suppose you get busy on your end of this deal."

Randall answered him, leaning toward the shorter man and speaking earnestly. But he had lowered his voice. Ken strained to hear, but the words were inaudible.

Suddenly Ken spotted a dark object on a table between himself and the long glass doors. He stifled an exclamation of excitement, and grabbed Sandy's arm. "Look!" he whispered. "A telephone!"

Sandy instinctively started toward it.

Bert grabbed him back. "Stay here!" Bert breathed. "You want to take the risk of being seen? The thing probably isn't even connected."

"But it's worth the chance of finding out," Ken insisted, softly. "I'll be careful." He dropped to his knees, ready to crawl around a long couch toward the table at the far end of it.

"But they'll hear you dial!" Bert whispered urgently.

"Go on, Ken," Sandy said. "He won't have to dial," he added to his brother.

Cautiously Ken moved forward, edging his way around the couch. Sandy was right. He wouldn't have to dial. He and Sandy had learned long ago that pressing the bar down softly, ten times, was equivalent to dialing the zero numeral that normally opened the line to the operator. But summoning the operator would be impossible if the telephone was not alive—or if he was seen trying to reach the instrument.

Now the table was only a few yards away.

Then he could stretch forth an arm and touch the table top.

An instant later, crouched between the table and a chair, Ken reached up and slowly lifted the phone from its cradle. Slowly he lowered his arm and pressed the instrument against his ear.

It was alive! The buzzing sound told him that.

With his other hand he reached up and felt for the bar on which it had rested. He depressed it once—twice—three times. . . . Counting to himself, keeping the pace of the depressions steady, he lowered the bar ten times in a row.

Then he waited, his heart thudding in his chest.

The voice of the operator on the other end of the line sounded so loud in his ear that he jumped. It seemed impossible that the men on the other side of the glass doors, only a few feet away, had not heard it too.

Ken cupped his hand around the mouthpiece and whispered into it. "Operator! Get me the Brentwood police! Quickly! This is a matter of life and death!"

"One moment, please!"

Ken swallowed.

On the other side of the doors Thorne's voice sounded once again. ". . . and that's the way we'll do it, Randall! That's. . . ."

The businesslike boom in Ken's ear cut off the rest of the angry speech. "Brentwood police. Canzoni speaking."

"Tony," Ken whispered, "this is Ken Holt. Let me talk to the chief. It's urgent!"

And then almost instantly Ken was connected with Chief Kane.

"Listen, Chief," Ken whispered. "We haven't much time. We're in a house with Frank Thorne. . . . Yes, Thorne! . . . No, I don't know where we are. But we've found a phone in the house here. It's dark. I can't see the number. Can you trace this call and get the address that way? . . . Good. . . . Yes, I'll leave the line open. . . . And—hurry, Chief! You'll have to get here fast if you're going to do any good. Hurry!"

Chief Kane was already busy tracing the call by the time Ken lowered the telephone softly to the rug, and started to crawl carefully back to where Bert and Sandy waited for him.

"Did you get him?" Sandy whispered.

The question relieved Ken's mind. If Sandy and Bert hadn't heard him, inside the room, he could feel sure he hadn't been heard by the men still standing outside the glass doors.

"Yes," Ken breathed quietly. "He's tracing the call. He'll be on his way as soon as he finds out where we are."

Sandy's big hand closed jubilantly on Ken's arm. "Now we—!" He broke off at the sound of activity beyond the glass.

"Get those doors open!" Thorne was commanding.

Immediately Chet and Vic bent over, in the glare of the flashlight, to raise the pair of slanting wooden doors that led down into the cellar.

"Get that tape off first," Thorne went on. "And do it carefully. Make sure you leave no marks. We want this to be a nice clean accident, with no loose ends to start people asking questions."

"We're not going to have much time," Bert said quietly. "The instant they're all out of sight in the cellar we've got to take off. We'd better head for the nearest patch of cover—not for our car. That's the first thing they'll check when they come out looking for us."

In the dimly lighted room Ken and Sandy nodded agreement. Bert was right. There wouldn't be time to find their car, start it, and take off. Sandy felt his coat pocket to make sure that his set of car keys were still there.

"Come on," Ken whispered, and started cautiously

forward toward the glass doors through which they meant to leave the house the instant the men had disappeared into the cellar.

Now the flashlight was aimed down the short flight of stairs revealed by the opening of the cellar entrance. Dan, Chet, and Vic moved down the steps in single file.

Ken stopped in his tracks.

Thorne and Randall were not following the other three men. They still stood at the top of the cellar stairs, their figures silhouetted against the light shining up from below.

They were talking quietly.

From where they stood, the glass doors for which Ken and Sandy and Bert had been heading were in plain sight.

"We can't get out!" Ken breathed.

Then they heard the bellow from the cellar.

"They're gone, boss. They got away!"

Thorne whirled to face the cellar entrance.

Dan tore up the stairs toward him, gun in hand. "They got away, boss!" he repeated furiously.

"But that's impossible!" Randall snapped. They must still be here! I saw their car at the front of the house when we drove up."

"Check it!" Thorne thrust Dan into motion. "Fast!"

Chet and Vic had reappeared too. Chet was flashing his light wildly around the landscape. "What'll we do?" he asked. "They could be any place out there! In that underbrush we'd need bloodhounds to—"

"Quiet!" Thorne commanded. "I'm thinking."

Dan came pounding back from the front of the house. "The car's still there! That means they're still—"

"It means," Thorne broke in flatly, "that they managed to get loose just about the time we arrived. They probably couldn't even get out of the house because we've been here." He grabbed the light out of Chet's hand and aimed it straight at the glass doors, flashing it back and forth. "They're probably still inside."

Ken dropped flat just before the beam knifed into the room. He could feel Bert and Sandy come down close at his heels.

Thorne's voice still came to them clearly.

"Chet, you'll stay right here," the man ordered, his voice grating roughly. "Dan, you get back to the front and guard the cars. Come on, Randall. You too, Vic. The first thing we'll do is search the house."

CHAPTER IX

A TRAP IS SPRUNG

AN instant later Thorne vanished down the cellar steps, with Randall and Vic at his heels.

The three figures in the dusky living room remained flat on the floor in motionless silence for a moment.

Then Sandy breathed, "If we crashed out through those glass doors and tackled Chet—"

"We'd never make it," his brother broke in, in a barely audible whisper. "He's got a gun."

None of them suggested attempting to break out through the front of the house. They knew Dan was on guard there, beside the cars.

Suddenly Ken said softly, "Those stairs going up out of the kitchen! Come on!"

Thorne had declared he meant to search the whole house, and Ken knew he would do just that. At that very moment, Ken realized, Thorne and the two men with him were exploring every inch of the cellar. Within minutes they would be on the first floor of the house. Eventually they would move up to the second floor. But if the Allens and he could avoid discovery for a little while yet. . . .

Ken was on his feet. Sandy and Bert had arisen too. Ken started back through the shadowy room, moving quietly on his toes and carefully avoiding the furniture in his path. Sandy and Bert were following behind him.

It was easier to find their way once they reached the kitchen. Ken crossed it in half a dozen strides. Once more he opened the door beyond which a flight of stairs led upward.

The stairs themselves were in total darkness.

Ken forced himself to slide his foot forward cautiously until it found the first step. "Keep to the edge," he whispered over his shoulder. "They may creak."

His groping hand found a stair rail, and he let it guide him. He tested each step before he let it take his weight, and was careful to keep as close as possible to the wall of the narrow stair well. His progress was soundless. Bert and Sandy, behind him, were also as silent as ghosts.

When Ken judged he must be close to the top of the flight, he stretched his free hand forward. If there was a door at the top of the stairs he didn't want to crash into it.

Below him, in the kitchen they had just left, a door opened.

"The kitchen," Thorne announced, his rough voice clearly audible to the three still feeling their way toward the second floor. "You stay right by this cellar door, Randall—in case they try to double back down there. Come on, Vic. You come with me."

Another door swung open, noisily, and Ken knew Thorne was entering the big shadowy living room with its long glass doors.

At that moment Ken's hand touched the solid wood of a door at the top of the stairs. He wasted a precious moment searching on the right side of it for a knob. He found what he was seeking on the door's left side.

With both hands he held the knob tight, and turned it slowly. The lock moved silently.

A voice only a few feet below them froze him where he stood. "Here's another door, boss!" Vic said.

Thorne's henchman jerked wide the door Bert had not dared to click shut, and a flash illuminated the first four steps of the flight. Just beyond the line of light Bert's figure held itself motionless. Sandy and Ken, above him, also held their breath.

"Stairs to the second floor!" Vic announced. "Want to go up, boss?"

"I said to come with me!" Thorne called from the living room. "The only way to search a place thoroughly is to take a floor at a time!"

"O.K." Vic sighed, and strode audibly across the

kitchen floor. "If we turned on some lights we could see—"

"No lights!" Thorne snapped. "This is supposed to be an empty house."

Cautiously, aware of Randall still close below them in the kitchen, Ken eased open the door at the top of the stairs. He stepped through it and to one side, still holding the doorknob. Sandy and Bert came through after him. Ken eased the door back into place, and turned the knob slowly until he could feel the lock click into place.

For what seemed like the first time in hours, they all took a deep breath. They had gained a temporary security. They had earned a few minutes of freedom, in which to search for a safe hiding place—or, better yet, a way out of the house.

With eyes that had grown accustomed to the dark, Ken could see that they stood on a small square landing. One step above them, and to the right, a wide hall ran toward the front of the house. Car headlights, which Dan had switched on, shone through a window at the corridor's far end.

To the left of the landing was a single door, slightly ajar.

Gently Ken pushed it farther open. Then he stepped through into what seemed to be a small room. He saw the gray rectangle of a window in its far wall and moved toward it.

A moment later he had returned to the landing.

"Bathroom," he whispered. "Window overlooks patio—where Chet's on guard."

There was no need for comment on his discovery. Sandy and Bert knew as well as Ken did that the bathroom window offered them no hope of escape.

In a silent group they turned their attention to the hall.

Its walls were punctured by three closed doors— two facing each other at the far end of the hall, one closer at hand.

Ken silently gestured toward the last. Sandy nodded, and pointed to the right-hand door farther away. Bert nodded too, and started for the third door as the boys moved toward the other two.

The room Ken entered was a bedroom, and so dark that he had to stand still for a moment before he could find the gray rectangle in the blackness which showed him the location of the single window. A rug beneath his feet muffled the sound of his steps, but he had to move cautiously to prevent himself from crashing into an unseen obstacle.

The window looked down into blackness, and for an instant Ken's heart rose. He pressed his face against the glass. If no one was on guard at this side of the house, and no lights shone here—

Then he turned away and a moment later made his way quietly back to the hall.

"Fifteen-foot drop into high shrubbery," he reported softly, when Bert and Sandy again stood beside him. "They'd hear us land—and be on us before we could get untangled and away."

Sandy reported on the room he had explored. "Two windows facing front over the porch roof. Easy drop to the roof—but Dan's on guard beside our car just below."

"Same situation in there," Bert whispered, jerking his head toward the third bedroom.

In the faint light of the corridor they stared at each other. They knew they could hide in one of the bedrooms—but they also knew that their hiding place would be discovered within a matter of minutes.

"Looks as if we've reached the end of the road," Sandy breathed. "And who knows when Kane will get here—if he ever does?"

"Wait!" Ken whispered. "There must be an attic!"

"But where's the stairway?" Bert asked.

"It ought to be over the one from the first floor," Ken began. Then he shook his head. They had explored the landing at the head of the stairs, and the bathroom that opened off it. If there had been a flight of attic stairs rising upward from that part of the second floor, they would have found it.

"In one of the rooms you were in?" Ken asked. He himself had examined the only door in the bedroom overlooking the shrubbery, and had found it to open on a small closet.

Two seconds were enough for Sandy and Bert to

report that the bedrooms they had examined also had only two doors each—one into the hall, the other into a closet.

Thorne's voice sounded suddenly from downstairs. "All right. They're not in this room. Now for—"

"Wait, boss! Here's a big closet!" Vic announced.

"Well, search it then—and make it fast!" Thorne ordered. "We haven't got a week, you know. Once an alarm goes out on that car, we may have trouble arranging that little accident."

Ken clenched his teeth. Their time was running out! On a desperate impulse he started toward the window at the end of the hall, with the vague thought that they might be able to drop to the porch roof and remain there out of sight until—

Something brushed across his face. He reached up instinctively to push away what he supposed was a cobweb. His hand closed around a piece of light rope dangling from overhead.

Ken stared up at it. Then he was pointing excitedly and Bert and Sandy were beside him, looking upward too.

"A trap door!" Ken breathed.

He didn't have to say more. In the Allen house, too, a trap door in the second-floor ceiling led upward into an attic. A pull on the rope dangling from the door lowered the door itself, on a slant, and permitted the folding stairway attached to its upper surface to slide down far enough to reach the floor.

Sandy grabbed Ken's arm. "We can barricade ourselves in up there! If we take the rope off, once we've got the stairs down—and then pull the stairs up after ourselves—they won't be able to get up after us!"

Ken nodded. "They may not even know the house has an attic!" Nothing Thorne or Randall had said, he remembered, indicated that they were familiar with the house they were using. Ken had already suspected that the men had simply borrowed a residence which they knew to be unoccupied.

Sandy reached for the rope, ready to jerk down the door.

Bert's hand closed on his arm before he could complete the gesture.

"Don't touch it!" Bert commanded in a whisper. "You know how much noise these things make!"

Sandy's hand fell back to his side. He and Ken looked at each other. Bert was right. The Allens' trap door, at any rate, creaked hideously when it was pulled down. It was safe to assume that most trap doors did the same.

And the first creak would bring Thorne, Vic, and Randall rushing up from the first floor, their guns at the ready.

Sandy's plan had seemed their one hope. Now it was clear that it offered no hope at all.

If only there was some way to prevent the trap door from making any noise as they—

Ken opened his mouth. "Noise!" he breathed. "That's it!"

Two pairs of eyes stared blankly into his.

"We can use the noise," Ken whispered hastily, "to trap them!"

"Trap them?" Sandy echoed.

"Yes! Listen!" Ken pulled their heads close. He knew he had no more than a few seconds in which to explain the plan that had suddenly occurred to him. He would have to talk fast. "We get them up into the attic—Thorne and Vic, I mean. Then we pile furniture under the trap door. Bureaus from the bedrooms. Then they can't open the door again to get out. D'you see? They can't push the stairs back down if something is holding the door shut. They'll be trapped up there!"

"It would work!" Sandy breathed excitedly.

"It might—if we could get them into the attic in the first place," Bert agreed.

"That's where the noise comes in," Ken whispered. "First we'll—" He was talking so rapidly now that his words ran together into a single whispered blur. But somehow the others understood him.

When the hasty explanation was concluded, Bert said, "It's a long shot. But let's try it."

"We've got to," Sandy agreed grimly.

"You take that bedroom down the hall then," Ken told him. "Get ready with the bureau there, but keep out of sight. Bert, you take the right front room. I'll duck into the other one as soon as I'm ready. And Bert—if Randall comes up too, to stand guard here—"

"I'll take care of him," Bert promised. "Just—"

He broke off and they all stood listening to the suddenly raised voice from downstairs.

". . . can't be down here, boss," Vic was saying. "So what now?"

"Upstairs of course!" Thorne snapped angrily. "Come on. You too, Randall."

"Get set!" Ken whispered.

Bert and Sandy were both moving silently away, each toward a bedroom door.

Ken reached up and took hold of the dangling rope. He waited until he heard the first footfall on the stairs rising from the first floor. Then he pulled.

The trap door began to open downward, its springs squeaking. A rattle sounded as the flight of steps attached to the upper side of the door began to slide into place.

Ken didn't let the steps reach the floor. When they were still at shoulder height he pushed them back upward, letting the springs pull the trap door back toward its closed position in the ceiling. It shut with a clatter that shook the house.

"What was that?" Thorne roared. But he answered his own question before the men with him had a chance to speak. "They're up there! Hurry!"

Three pairs of feet were pounding up from the

first floor, making the enclosed stairway echo like a drum.

Ken ducked into the front bedroom opposite the one where Bert was hidden.

Behind him, in the hall, the rope was still swinging from the vigorous sideways jerk he had given it at the last moment.

A door banged open.

"Not in here!" Vic's voice said an instant later.

From its direction Ken knew Vic had flashed his light into the bathroom opening off the landing at the head of the stairs.

"Only three more rooms up here!" Vic said triumphantly an instant later, as footsteps sounded in the hall. "It won't be long now, boss!"

"Hold it!" Thorne said, more quietly than he had spoken since the boys' disappearance from the cellar had been discovered. "They're not in any of those rooms, Vic. Use your head. Look at that rope dangling from the ceiling. It's still swinging!"

"Huh? Oh, yeah—I see it. But what—?"

"And see that rectangle above it?" Thorne went on. "That's a trap door into the attic. They've just used it. That was the noise we heard—that trap door closing."

"But how'd they get up there, boss?" Vic sounded puzzled. "I don't see a ladder or—"

"There's a flight of stairs on the inner side of that door," Thorne told him impatiently. "They slide down when— But never mind that now. The point is they're up there. The stupid fools!" There was a note of scornful amusement in the rough voice. "They get out of one trap and walk right into another one!"

Ken heard a creak and a rattle. He knew Thorne was pulling the dangling rope.

"Say! Look at that!" Vic muttered.

The base of the trap door stairs thumped against the floor.

Thorne raised his voice. "All right—you up there!" he called. "Your little game of hide-and-seek is over. You can come down now!"

Complete silence was his only answer.

Thorne waited for perhaps fifteen seconds. Then he spoke again.

"You'll be sorry for this!" he barked. "I'll give you one more chance—and then I'll come up and get you. I'll count to three. Either you're heading down these stairs by the time I say three or—! One! Two! Three!"

Again there was no response but utter silence.

"All right!" Thorne said furiously. "Vic, you come with me. You stay here, Randall, in case they try to duck around us up there."

His heavy footfall sounded on the stairway. Vic's lighter tread followed.

Ken held his rigid pose behind the bedroom door until both pairs of feet landed on the solid attic floor.

I'll make you pay for this time you're costing me!"

Thorne's voice was saying, as Ken made his first move.

Cautiously he peered through the crack in the door he had left slightly ajar. Randall stood only three feet away, his back to Ken, his head tilted up toward the opening in the ceiling.

"There's a lot of stuff up here, boss!" Vic muttered.

"I can see that for myself!" Thorne told him angrily. "You take that side. I'll take this. They may try to make a break for it!" he added, raising his voice. "Keep a sharp eye out down there, Randall."

Ken saw the crack in the opposite door, and knew that Bert was just behind it, ready to strike.

The time had come.

Ken jerked the door wide with his left hand, pushed his right arm through the opening in the same instant, and tapped Randall on the shoulder.

The man jumped and spun around. His eyes stared straight into Ken's. His mouth opened.

But he made no sound. Bert was already behind him. The board-hard edge of Bert's hand struck the side of Randall's neck.

The open mouth twisted in a silent grimace of pain. The staring eyes glazed.

For an instant Randall's body swayed like an erratic pendulum. The short length of pipe he held in his hand slipped from his nerveless grasp. Bert caught it before it crashed to the floor.

Ken knew that Bert was ready to strike

Then Randall's legs turned liquid. His knees buck-led. His head flopped forward.

Ken and Bert, between them, eased him to the floor.

"O.K.," Ken breathed. Bert disappeared instantly back into the bedroom.

Ken's mouth was dry. Everything depended on the next few seconds.

He pulled Randall's limp body out of the way, against the wall.

By the time he straightened Sandy was in sight in the open door of the bedroom toward the rear of the house. The redhead's powerful arms held a three-drawer chest clear of the floor. He had taken the drawers out of it to lighten it, but even so his set face showed the strain of the weight as he slowly carried his burden closer.

Ken crossed to the doorway through which Bert had disappeared. It too was open now, but partly blocked by a high bureau.

Ken took one side of it. Bert took the other. They picked it up and eased it over the threshold. Once out in the hall, it stood only a few feet away from the trap-door stairway.

Ken glanced toward Sandy. It was all right. He was close enough.

Ken took hold of the bottom of the folding stair-way and heaved.

The lower half flipped up and folded back toward

the upper half. Before it came to rest, Ken shoved hard again. The whole mechanism moved upward, fast. The trap door slammed shut with a crash.

A split second later Thorne was bellowing, "Randall! Randall! Open that door! What's going on—"

The boys weren't listening to him.

Ken and Bert were pushing the tall bureau into place just under the trap door, with a single mighty shove. Then they turned toward Sandy. With timing as accurate as if it had been rehearsed for hours, their three pairs of hands hoisted the three-drawer chest to the top of the bureau. It landed with a thud.

All three of them looked upward.

The top of the chest was only six inches below the ceiling—only six inches below the trap door.

Even as they looked, the trap door was thrust downward. It banged noisily against the chest and stopped.

Through the slitlike opening between the end of the trap door and the ceiling Thorne's voice raged. "Randall! Open this door! Randall!"

Again his voice went unheeded.

Bert and Sandy had picked up Randall's still-unconscious figure and were carrying it swiftly toward the flight of stairs that led down to the first floor. With his shoulder Sandy pushed shut the door at the head of the stairs, and then they rolled Randall's body against it.

By the time they joined Ken in the right front

bedroom, overlooking the porch roof, Ken had the window open.

Dan was visible below, still standing where he had been posted, beside the boys' convertible. But now Dan was staring upward toward the house, stabbing his flashlight first toward one window and then toward another.

"Boss!" he was calling softly, his voice thin with uncertainty. "What's happened? What's going on?"

His partner, Chet, joined him on the run. "What's up?" he asked quickly. "I thought I heard the boss yelling. Something must have—"

Two quick shots came from the attic. Then two more shots followed. Plaster dust billowed out through the hall.

"Randall! Chet! Dan!" Thorne shouted, and a heavy foot thudded against the trap door that would not open.

The two guards below leaped into action. This time they had heard the roaring voice. One behind the other they raced toward the corner of the house and disappeared from sight, on their way to the one doorway of the house that seemed to be open —the cellar doorway.

"Let's go!" Ken said.

He crawled through the open window onto the porch roof, and moved swiftly aside so that Sandy and Bert could follow. An instant later they were all dangling by their hands from the edge of the roof, in the full glare of their own headlights. Raging words followed through the open window behind them.

"We're locked in the attic! Get us out!" That time the voice was Vic's.

"No!" Thorne yelled. "Stop them! Find them! Don't let them get away!"

Ken, Sandy, and Bert dropped to the ground.

"Got your set of keys, Sandy?" Ken asked swiftly.

"Sure."

"Start the car then and take it fifty feet down the lane. We'll join you there. Come on, Bert. Let's smash the headlights of their cars so they can't chase us too fast!"

As he spoke, he picked up a brick from the border of a flower bed, handed it to Bert, and grabbed another for himself.

Bert headed for the truck. Ken moved toward the car parked beside it.

Their blows coincided. One! Two!

The crashes were still echoing as they dropped their bricks, spun around, and started to run.

Ahead of them two red stop lights broke the blackness, stayed alive for a second, and then disappeared.

Immediately a flashlight beam stabbed downward from the window at the end of the second-floor hall. It aimed at the spot where the convertible had stood a moment earlier, wavered, and then moved in crazy erratic arcs.

"Down!" Bert pulled Ken off the driveway and against the waist-high shrubbery that bordered it. "Crawl!" he said. "It's only another twenty feet."

"Find them!" Thorne was still raging from the attic. "Find them! Shoot them!"

"But we can't—! There's nothing to shoot at!"

"Don't stay in the house, you idiots!" Thorne yelled. "Get outside and chase them! If they get away—!"

Ken couldn't see where he was going. Branches lashed across his face. Sharp stones cut into his hands and knees.

"Ken—Bert!" Sandy's whisper was loud in the darkness. "Here!"

Ken bumped into something solid. His groping fingers closed around something hard and curved.

And then he was on his feet, stumbling around to the side of the car and hurling himself through the open door. Bert landed beside him.

"Go!" Bert gasped.

Sandy eased the car forward, feeling his way in the blackness. The road curved. He rounded the bend.

Then he flicked on the headlights and stepped down hard. With the white rays lighting the way ahead, the car roared down the bumpy lane.

Half a minute later Sandy jammed on the brake. The lane had ended at a junction with a country road. To the right—to the left—there were no lights, no sign of habitation.

"Which way?" Sandy asked.

"Listen!" Ken said.

They all heard it then—the sound of a siren's wail, rising and falling but growing steadily louder, somewhere off toward their left.

In the dim glow of the light from the instrument panel they looked at each other.

"I guess we don't have to go either way," Sandy said. There was the beginning of a grin in his voice.

"I guess not," Ken agreed. "We can wait right here for Andy Kane—and a nice little story for Pop and Global News."

CHAPTER X

TAKING STOCK

THE clock on the office wall said half-past five. The first light of dawn was graying the big front window, silhouetting the letters that spelled out BRENTWOOD ADVANCE. From overhead the harsh glare of electric light beat down on five people.

Andy Kane slumped in the visitor's chair beside Pop's battered desk behind which Pop himself was wearily stuffing his pipe.

Bert had slid so far down in his seat that only his head and shoulders could be seen behind his ancient typewriter. His face still showed the marks of the blow Dan's fist had landed on it some four hours earlier.

Ken and Sandy appeared to be entrenched behind a bulwark of empty coffee containers and crumpled sandwich wrappers heaped on Ken's desk.

Sandy yawned. "I guess we've said all there is to say," he muttered unnecessarily. "And eaten all there is to eat," he added. He reached for a coffee container, stared into it, shook his head sadly, and put it down again.

"Have this one." Bert's long arm stretched out toward his brother, offering him a container of coffee that had not yet been opened.

"Thanks!" Sandy brightened as he reached to accept it. An instant later he frowned. "It's cold!" he complained.

"What did you expect?" Ken asked him. "The last batch of supplies the diner sent over arrived an hour ago."

The phone rang. Pop scooped it up, said "Brentwood Advance," listened for a moment, and then handed the instrument to the chief of police.

"Kane here," the chief said. "Go ahead." He nodded slowly as he listened. When he handed the phone back to Pop he spoke to the boys and Bert. "That house they were holding you in belongs to some people named Jenkins. They use it only week ends. They're not involved in this at all." He sighed. "But they sure made it easy for Thorne's men. They left a note for the milkman telling him to deliver milk this coming Saturday, and saying that they'd pay him when they arrived for the week end. With that note, anybody could see the place would be empty until then."

Pop picked up a pencil. "How'd Thorne and Randall happen to pick it?" he asked, and prepared to add notes to those he had already taken.

"His men spotted it when they followed Ken and Sandy to the auction yesterday," Kane explained. "They were looking for a place to take the boys to after they kidnaped them—a place nearby so as to avoid transporting them any distance in daytime. The house had the look of an empty place, and when they drove up to investigate, and found the note in the milk bottle, they knew they were all set. It's only a couple of miles from the Pollard farm, you know, and they had plenty of time to find it and come back to the auction to wait for you, while you were doing your job there."

"We know now that it's close to Pollard's," Ken said, grinning wearily. "But when we were tied up in that cellar we were ready to swear there wasn't a human being within fifty miles."

"Make it a hundred," Sandy said.

Once more the room lapsed into silence.

"Funny thing," Pop murmured, "a slick operator like Randall getting involved with a strong-arm thug like Thorne!"

"Randall's skated pretty close to the edge of the law himself, Pop," Bert reminded him. "I was checking on him in the morgue. Half a dozen of his stock deals were so shady that he barely squeaked by without a prison sentence."

"Still—it's kind of strange."

"It'll be strange if I can stay awake another five minutes," Sandy said, yawning again. "I wish those two big wheels from the Petrane Oil Company would get here so we could learn the rest of the story." He yawned once more. "And get to bed," he added.

"The rest of the story?" Ken echoed. "We don't know much of anything yet—except that some clerk in the Petrane office stole the mimeograph stencils of a geologist's report, tried to pass them to one of Thorne's men in the garage of the Global News building, got panicky when he saw police searching the place, and stashed the envelope in our car instead. All very interesting, of course," he added, "especially what happened to us as a result. But we still haven't the slightest glimmer of what it's really all about."

"And maybe we won't find out tonight," Pop said. "It's hard to believe that a couple of big oil executives would get up in the middle of the night and drive out here to Brentwood—"

"Is it, Pop?" Bert broke in. "Then you're going to have to make a big effort. Because here they are now."

They all looked through the front window then, at the long black limousine that had just stopped at the curb outside. A uniformed chauffeur jumped out, came around to the rear door of the car, and opened it.

The two passengers who stepped out, one after the other, did not look like the type of men who normally got up before dawn. They were perfectly groomed, in spite of the fact that they had been roused from their beds some three hours earlier, driven from New York to Brentwood, and had been in session with Judge Brayton at the Brentwood courthouse for the past hour.

Pop stood up as they entered the office. "Mr. Cruikshank?" He looked inquiringly from one to the other. "Mr. Weldon?"

"I'm Cruikshank." The man in dark gray walked across the room and extended his hand. "And this is Weldon, head of Petrane's legal staff." He was looking curiously as he spoke at Bert and the boys. "And you, I assume, are the near victims of the Thorne-Randall combination?"

"Let's get at the Petrane Company's story on this crime—or crimes," Pop said, when the introductions had been completed. "We've got a lot of holes to fill in."

"In good time, sir. In good time." Weldon opened the attaché case he carried, took out a pad of paper, and then closed the case to use it as a writing board. "First we would like to have the full names of the three near victims. As you will learn, in good time, they have done a most valuable service to the company—a service that we feel should not go unrewarded. As chairman of the board, Mr. Cruikshank" —he nodded deferentially toward his companion— "is fully empowered to act in this regard."

"Look, Mr. Weldon," Bert said, " we haven't been

trying to win a reward. We weren't even trying to do anything for Petrane. We got out of that mess because we wanted to save our necks. But now we would kind of like to know what's in that envelope —what makes those stencils so valuable to you and to Thorne and Randall too."

Cruikshank smiled pleasantly. "I'm afraid you're being too modest," he said. "After all, it was thanks to you that the police were able to apprehend those men. For that alone you should have some sort of reward. Furthermore," he went on, "it was a Petrane employee—in custody now, may I add, and confessing freely—who put that envelope in your car and thus involved you in an unfortunate and dangerous series of events. Under the circumstances we feel that our firm owes you a reward if only as a gesture of apology."

"Gentlemen," Pop said, with an edge of impatience in his voice, "this happens to be a weekly paper and today happens to be our press day. Furthermore, those two"—he indicated Ken and Sandy—"have a commitment to Global News to supply an account of the night's events. So what we need now—all of us— is the kernel of the story. So far as a reward is concerned," he added hastily, when the Petrane legal representative seemed about to make another speech, "nobody will quarrel over that. If I know these boys —and I do—they'll be happy to accept any reward you care to make them, with the understanding that it will be turned over to some worth-while Brentwood project—the library, the hospital, the children's recreation center. . . . And now if we might get to the facts."

"Very commendable," Cruikshank said. "Of course the reward will be handled in accordance with the recipients' wishes. Unfortunately, sir," he went on to Pop, "I am afraid that I cannot honor your request for information about the contents of that envelope. We came here to express our gratitude, and to make arrangements to give that gratitude a more concrete form."

"I don't understand," Pop said, after a startled pause. "You say that three reporters of my paper did your company an invaluable service. Yet you also say, in effect, that you cannot let them know what that service was."

"Precisely." Cruikshank raised his hands as if to indicate helplessness. "If I were to divulge the contents of that envelope—let the world know the information contained in those stencils—I would myself be destroying the entire value of the service done for us. The material on those stencils must remain a secret for the time being."

Pop glanced at Andy. "Those stencils are being held as evidence, aren't they?"

Cruikshank spoke before Kane could answer. "On Judge Brayton's order," he said, "they have been impounded." Again he smiled. "I understand your interest," he said, "but I'm afraid you will not be permitted to see them in any case."

Pop took a deep breath. "Mr. Cruikshank," he said evenly, "I must assume that from your point of view you have a good reason for refusing our request. But what you may consider a good reason, speaking for the Petrane Company, may not appear quite so good to a newspaper editor who feels he has a duty to the public. I do not intend to muzzle my paper on your say-so. Suppose I print the full story of the night's events—including your refusal to co-operate," he suggested. "Don't you think that the legitimate public curiosity that would be aroused in that case might do your company more harm than the full story, freely told?"

"You can't flout a court order!" Weldon said angrily. "We'll get an injunction to stop you."

"Come, Mr. Weldon," Pop said. "Talk sense. What court would give you an injunction to stop a paper's own reporters from reporting events in which they were involved? And those events include," he added pointedly, "certain fragments of conversation between Thorne and Randall."

Cruikshank smiled wryly. "Weldon," he said, "you can't bluff Mr. Allen." He looked at Bert and the boys, and then back to Pop. "I'm going to tell you what's in those stencils," he said abruptly.

"Mr. Cruikshank!" Weldon protested.

"Leave this to me, Weldon," Cruikshank said

firmly. "I'm going to tell them—and leave it up to their own judgment as to whether the story should be printed immediately or not."

"Good," Pop said. "I can speak for my crew. We appreciate your confidence. And I think you can trust our judgment. You understand," he added quickly, "I am not speaking for Chief Kane here. If he needs evidence—"

"Don't worry, Chief," Cruikshank said quickly. "You'll have our evidence in this affair when it is needed." He paused to take a deep breath, and then he plunged in.

"Petrane is a petroleum producer, as you know," he began. "Recently we have had a survey team operating in the Middle East, prospecting on a large area of land we have leased there. Our geologists completed their report three weeks ago. Thorne and Randall—we know now—tried to buy that report, and failed. They then won the co-operation of one of our clerks, Amos Slater—the man you say you bumped into in the basement," he told Ken and Sandy. "For the sum of five thousand dollars, according to Slater's confession, he agreed to make the report available to Thorne and Randall. He knew that the report was to be mimeographed for our board of directors. Normally it would be his duty to destroy the stencils when the job was done. In this case he slipped them into an envelope—still sticky and inky, as they came off the machine—and went down into the cellar garage where he had arranged to turn them over to one of Thorne's henchmen."

Cruikshank's grim face lighted briefly as he murmured. "As you know by now, of course, our offices occupy two floors in the building that also houses Global News."

Then he sobered again and went on. "I don't need to tell you what happened to that envelope. Slater panicked when he saw police searching the garage. When you two left him to question the police, he put the envelope in your car. Then he went outside and told Thorne's henchmen what he had done, so that you could be followed until the envelope was retrieved. The rest of the story you know better than we do.

"The report itself, however, is what you wish to know about," Cruikshank was speaking more slowly. "But let me see if you will not agree with me when I say that it could have serious consequences for many people, if it were released at this time to the public. If word gets out that Petrane has—let us say for the sake of argument—discovered a rich new field, Petrane stock would soar immediately. If, on the other hand, it were to become known that our leased lands were worthless, our stocks would tumble. Either way," he concluded, "a smart and unscrupulous man like Randall could speculate and make a tremendous profit."

Ken was puzzled. "But the report will be announced eventually—won't it?" he asked. "Whether it's good or bad, you don't expect to keep it a secret forever."

"Of course not," Cruikshank said quickly. "We simply want the report to go first to our stockholders. They have the right to know first. I'll tell you one thing more. The report is—well, let's say promising. When it is issued we will give our stockholders the first opportunity to buy the new issue of shares we plan to offer. Each stockholder will be permitted to buy one new share at a low price, for each two he already owns." He paused. "Do you see now," he asked, "what a shrewd operator like Randall could do if he knew about that report a day or even a few hours before the stockholders were aware of it? He could buy thousands of Petrane shares in the market, from unknowing stockholders—because he would know that his purchase would give him the opportunity to buy half that number of shares of the new issue at half of what those shares will be worth in a few weeks. Why, he could clean up thousands of dollars —at our stockholders' expense!"

"Thorne said Randall had promised they would split a million," Sandy said.

"Exactly! I wouldn't be surprised if unscrupulous people could clear that amount—or even more," Cruikshank declared. For the first time in many minutes he leaned back in his chair. "Now do you see," he asked, "why we can't let this story out?"

The office of the *Advance* was silent for a moment.

"No," Ken said then, "I just don't see what damage the story would do." He looked directly at the chairman of the board of directors. "I don't know anything about the stock market," he went on, "but it seems to me there's something lacking in what you've told us. I think you've left something out. Or," he added, "that you're still trying to bluff us."

"I agree," Pop said quickly. "From what you've told us so far, I don't see what harm a story about tonight's events—including a description of that geological report—could do."

"Look, Mr. Cruikshank," Ken said, leaning forward. "You've told us your report was—well, promising, you said. So suppose we publish that fact. What would happen? Seems to me the result would be that Petrane stock would rise. But everybody would know the facts. It would rise because it had become more valuable in the eyes of the public. Your stockholders could sell if they wanted to—but they couldn't be tricked into selling. They'd have read the story too. So how could they be tricked—as you say they might —by some smart operator like Randall? And we *know* they couldn't be tricked by Randall now," he added. "He's out of the picture."

Cruikshank sighed. He looked toward Ken and then away again. "You're a smart young man," he said finally. "I suppose that I might as well tell you the—"

"Mr. Cruikshank!" Weldon broke in swiftly. "Don't! Don't admit anything!"

"Weldon," Cruikshank said wearily, "if they print their own report of what happened to them tonight, without any background material from us, that would be the most damaging thing that could happen. And we haven't been able to convince them to keep silent in view of—what was it you called it, Mr. Allen?—your duty to the public? All right, gentlemen. We're at your mercy."

The man looked slowly around the circle of faces—Pop's, Bert's, Chief Kane's, Sandy's, and Ken's. "I said that report was promising," he repeated slowly. "And it is. But the most promising field our geological team found was just outside the area we have leased. The men had crossed the boundary of that area by accident. They were following traces of oil in our own land—and realized suddenly that the best oil source was just outside that territory. We are now trying to lease the land which their survey proved to be the most promising. Our negotiations have been going on for three weeks. We have every reason to believe they will be successful.

"In fact," Cruikshank said with a faint smile, "I was sure it was a call from the Middle East which woke me up a few hours ago. Instead, it was the terrifying information that our report had fallen into the hands of—"

He stopped, as if he could not go on. A moment later he added quietly, "And that's the truth of our difficult situation, gentlemen. If it comes out within the next few hours, before our lease goes through, other companies will be bidding for that land—big companies that can outbid us a dozen times over. Petrane stock will go down. Petrane stockholders will lose millions. But if you hold your story until we sign that lease," he added, his voice strengthening, "you will lose nothing but a few hours—and you will save a good company from near-ruin."

Pop slowly selected a match from the holder on his desk. Deliberately he scratched it on the underside of his desk. Carefully he applied it to his dead pipe. Over the flame he looked from Bert to Sandy to Ken. "What do you think?" he asked. "After all, this is your story."

Ken spoke first. "I think we ought to hold off, Pop," he said firmly.

"I agree," Bert said. He grinned suddenly. "After all, I've had one good thing out of this situation already. I got a good poke at Randall."

"It's all right with me," Sandy said. "On one condition," he added.

"Name it," Cruikshank said. "You have us over that well-known barrel, gentlemen. We won't refuse anything within reason."

"That we get first and exclusive crack at the story

when you can release it," Sandy said. He winked at Ken. "I want the pleasure of letting Granger know once more what good reporters we are."

Cruikshank let out his breath in a great sigh. "Your condition is met," he said. "With our gratitude. And speaking of gratitude," he went on more briskly, and smiling again, "let's come to some agreement about that reward now. I didn't want to press you on the amount earlier. I didn't want you to think we were trying to bribe you."

"I've got the papers right here, Mr. Cruikshank," Weldon said quickly, opening his attaché case. "If you'd care to fill in an amount right now, and add your signature—"

The shrill jangle of the phone interrupted him.

Pop picked up the instrument. *"Brentwood Advance.* Allen speaking." He listened briefly. "For you," he said then, handing the phone to Cruikshank.

"Thank you." The executive spoke his name. "Oh, yes, Jackson!" he said. "Yes, go ahead." He listened without saying a word for full half a minute. Slowly the lines in his face smoothed out.

"You're certain?" he said finally. "There's no chance of a slip-up? . . . Good! . . . What? . . . No!" The single syllable burst from him like an explosion and he straightened in his chair. "Absolutely not! You will say not a word! This story will be released from here—from Brentwood!"

For a moment he listened to the crackling speech

coming over the line. Then he broke in. "I know it's irregular, Jackson," he said. "But this whole business has been irregular, to put it mildly. Remember now— not one word, if you value your job. Thanks for calling, Jackson," he added more calmly.

He put the phone back in its cradle and turned smiling to his audience. "Gentlemen," he said, "the story is yours—first and exclusive. Our lease is signed!"

Sandy leaped up. "Don't move, Mr. Cruikshank!" he said. "I want to get a picture!"

"Oh, no!" Weldon rose too, in obvious distress. "Mr. Cruikshank never permits his picture to be used in the papers! Never!"

The chairman of the board of directors reached out a hand and jerked Weldon down into his chair again. "Mr. Cruikshank," he said, "will have his picture in the papers tomorrow morning—in the *Brentwood Advance* and in any other publication to which our friends here care to submit it. And what's more, Weldon," he added, "Mr. Cruikshank is going to like it!"

Bert was sliding a fresh sheet of paper into his typewriter. "What do you expect the new field to yield, Mr. Cruikshank?" he asked.

"What about your clerk?" Ken was on his feet, a wad of copy paper in his hand. "Are you pressing charges against him for—?"

Cruikshank waved his hand feebly. "What is this?"

he asked. "When we walked in here not long ago you all looked as if you were about to go to sleep for a week. Now you're all popping off like a bunch of sparklers!"

Pop laughed. "Of course they are," he said. "You've just given them a shot of newsman's oxygen —the whiff of an important story."

"Important!" Sandy echoed scornfully. "Why, we'll never get a better one!"

But as usual Sandy's enthusiasm was leading him into error. There was a better story in the offing— a better story that would follow the grim adventure which came to be known as *The Mystery of the Plumed Serpent*.